P9-DCB-903

THE IMAGE OF LOVE

It wouldn't be long now. Until then, as Lady Louisa had said, Gideon would have to learn patience.

He left the dining room and mounted the stairs of the large manor house, pausing at the painting as he always did. He looked around to be certain that he was alone. Finch had caught him gazing raptly at Lady Elizabeth one day and had looked at him very strangely.

At the moment, no one was about, and he stepped as close as he could to the image of the beautiful girl on the chestnut horse. Dark, lustrous curls hung loose to her waist. Her large eyes glowed with amusement. He could almost hear her laughter.

"Soon," he murmured.

Other Novels by Julia Parks

FORTUNE'S FOOLS

TO MARRY AN HEIRESS

A GIFT FOR A ROGUE

HIS SAVING GRACE

THE DEVIL AND MISS WEBSTER

Published by Zebra Books

Marriage Minded

Julia Parks

ZEBRA BOOKS
Kensington Publishing Corp.
www.kensingtonbooks.com

ZEBRA BOOKS are published by

Kensington Publishing Corp.
850 Third Avenue
New York, NY 10022

Copyright © 2005 by Donna Bell

All rights reserved. No part of this book may be reproduced in any form or by any means without the prior written consent of the Publisher, excepting brief quotes used in reviews.

If you purchased this book without a cover you should be aware that this book is stolen property. It was reported as "unsold and destroyed" to the Publisher and neither the Author nor the Publisher has received any payment for this "stripped book."

All Kensington titles, imprints and distributed lines are available at special quantity discounts for bulk purchases for sales promotion, premiums, fund-raising, educational or institutional use.

Special book excerpts or customized printings can also be created to fit specific needs. For details, write or phone the office of the Kensington Special Sales Manager: Kensington Publishing Corp., 850 Third Avenue, New York, NY 10022. Attn. Special Sales Department. Phone: 1-800-221-2647.

Zebra and the Z logo Reg. U.S. Pat. & TM Off.

First Printing: April 2005
10 9 8 7 6 5 4 3 2 1

Printed in the United States of America

To Mrs. Giggleplump's favorite grandchildren:
Hallie, Truman, and Amanda.

Chapter One

"Hurry, Captain! She's goin' down!"

Gideon only shook his head and ducked into the passageway that led to his quarters. Throwing open the door, he rushed inside and grabbed the precious box that contained his ship's log. A deafening crack rent the air and threw him against the wall. Bracing himself, he paused for a split second before dashing out the door.

It was then that he noticed the closed door where his sole passenger was lodged. Surely the man had gotten out. Gideon started down the narrow corridor that led to safety. Lord Winters couldn't have slept through all that . . . still, both of them had dipped deeply in the bottle at dinner.

Gideon retraced his steps and opened the cabin door. There was the dandy, lying on the floor, blood covering his face. With a curse, Gideon bent over him. Feeling the steady pulse, he hoisted the unconscious figure over his shoulder and ran for safety.

Boswell had waited, thank God. The lifeboat was still lashed to the limping ship's side. Gideon threw the unconscious man inside the boat and leaped after him as his first officer cut the ropes and set them free.

"I think this will be the one, Cordelia, I really do."

"I have ceased counting on it, Louisa. How many has she turned down over the years? It must be two dozen."

"Surely not," said the gentler Lady Louisa.

"I cannot say for certain, of course. There may very well have been others she has turned down, some we do not know of."

"Well, thank heavens dear Sir Landon has finally presented himself. I believe our Elizabeth has been waiting for him all this time. Really, I do. I mean, she has known him since childhood. You remember how she was always trying to tag along when he and Avery were out adventuring."

"True," said the formidable Lady Rotherford. "I do hope you are right. At six and twenty, if Elizabeth does not wed this Season, she will be firmly on the shelf despite her fortune."

"And her beauty," said Lady Louisa. "Let us not forget that the gentlemen set great store . . . by . . . oh, dear . . ." she whispered in despair, half rising from her chair before sinking back down.

The handsome Sir Landon Wakefield strode past the elderly ladies without a word. Before either lady could speak, a composed Lady Elizabeth Winters strolled into the room, took the chair next to the sofa where her stunned grandmothers sat, and poured a cup of tea.

Holding up the pot, she asked, "Would either of you like another cup?"

"Oh, Elizabeth! Not Sir Landon? Surely there is nothing to object to in Sir Landon!" whined Lady Louisa.

Her other grandmother, the Countess of Rotherford, rounded on her only granddaughter with a tart, "You are impossible to please, Elizabeth! What, pray tell, could have put you off Sir Landon? He is handsome, charming, and his fortune, though it may not match yours, is quite respectable."

"Quite respectable," echoed her other grandmother. "And handsome. So very handsome. I mean, my dear, haven't you noticed those broad shoulders and muscular calves?" When the countess cleared her throat,

Lady Louisa colored up and stammered, "I simply mean to say that Sir Landon is a splendid choice for a husband."

"Indeed, yes, perfectly splendid," said the countess.

Taking a deep breath, Elizabeth put her cup and saucer on the silver tray and smoothed her skirts. Her smile was fixed as she repeated, "Splendid? Why would you call him splendid? Because he has killed enough men to be knighted for his military service? Perhaps it is because he has bedded more females in the two months he has been back in England than any other man returned from the war?"

"Elizabeth!"

"No? Well, I know it cannot be because of all the wonderful works he has done to help the poor or to repair the problems in our ailing society, since he has not done one thing of worth since returning to England. Now, if you will excuse me, I must collect the baskets Cook was making up for the poor and distribute them." Elizabeth rose, bent to kiss the cheeks each of her grandmothers offered her, and walked regally out the door.

When she was gone, Lady Rotherford expelled a breath and chuckled. At her companion's quizzical look, she said, "She is magnificent, isn't she? I mean, I would see her settled, but I cannot imagine a man who could match her."

"But Sir Landon . . ."

"No, he is not her equal. Had she accepted the likable rogue, she would have died of boredom in six months. I cannot imagine the two of them sitting by the fire of a night, can you?"

"No, I suppose not. But, Cordelia, Elizabeth must wed. How else can she be happy?"

"How indeed?" murmured the countess. "There is nothing for it, Louisa. We must continue to throw men at her head this coming Season until she settles on one. We will not rest until our dear Elizabeth is wed!"

* * *

"Good afternoon, m'dear. Have you been to see Mrs. Plunkett?"

From her seat on the dogcart, Elizabeth smiled down at the speaker, a stern-looking man of some sixty-eight years, and nodded. "Yes, Grandfather, and she said to tell you that she still has the best hens in the parish."

"And did she give you some of her eggs to prove it?" he asked, placing his hands on her waist and swinging her easily to the ground.

"Of course. They are rather large, Grandfather. Larger than ours here at Wintersford, I'm afraid," said Elizabeth.

"I shall have to bring in some more hens, I suppose. Can't let it get about the country that Mrs. Plunkett has bested me."

They laughed, and Elizabeth took his arm while one of the grooms led her pony and trap away.

Strolling toward the house, the earl asked, "How is the old dame?"

"I fear she hasn't long, Grandfather. She looks very drawn, and even her laugh has lost its heartiness."

"I shall have to pay her a visit tomorrow. It is difficult to imagine Wintersford without our Mrs. Plunkett."

Elizabeth gave his arm a consoling squeeze, and her grandfather placed his hand over hers. She glanced at the pronounced veins and the brown spots on the back of his hand and frowned.

Nothing escaped the shrewd old earl, and he said, "We all grow older."

A squeak of protest escaped before she could prevent it, and Elizabeth said fiercely, "Not you, Grandfather. You will always be here."

He laughed, and the sound came out loud and strong. "Do not get me wrong, my child. I am hardly packing my bag for my own trip right now."

Elizabeth breathed a sigh of relief. Her world without

him was unthinkable. Her grandfather had always been there to pick her up and dust her off. She had been only three when her father and uncle had been killed in the carriage accident. Her grandfather had stepped into the role of father to her and her cousin Avery. She could not remember when he had not been there to share her laughter and her tears.

"There will be a time, however . . ."

His brow was furrowed as he searched for words. Looking into his dark brown eyes, Elizabeth felt a chill run the length of her spine.

"I only mention it, my dear, because I would like to part this world knowing that you were settled and happy. I would even like to be able to dandle your own infant on my knee."

"Grandfather! You sound like Grandmother and Mimi."

"I know, I know, and I have been loath to press the matter. I must confess that I like having you here with us. Besides which, I thought they would be able to persuade you, so I left the chore to them, but it seems they have failed miserably in helping you settle on a husband."

With a toss of her dark brown curls, she said, "I do not intend to *settle* on anyone."

His brow formed deep furrows as he led her to a nearby arbor, where he pulled her down to sit by his side. Secluded from the world, he asked, "Why? Why have you been unable to choose a husband, child? I know it is not from a lack of offers. I have dealt with more offers than I care to remember. Of course, I was not surprised when you turned down Sir Landon. He was not the one for you, but there have been others more worthy than him. Could you not love one of them?"

Elizabeth shuffled her feet. It had always been thus. Whenever she had displeased him, he had taken her to one side and asked her to explain herself, all the while keeping his temper completely in check. She wished she possessed the same patience and forbearance.

She could not keep the petulance from her voice as she replied, "I haven't met the man I can love. It is as simple as that."

"But what sort of man are you looking for?"

"I . . . I don't know, Grandfather," she said, her own frustration evident in her tone. "I want someone who is neither a fool, nor a tyrant."

"Like your stepfather," he remarked astutely.

"Perhaps tyrant is too harsh a word, because I know my mother loves him and chooses to allow him to make all those awful decisions that keep his own son in poverty."

"Your half brother Val is impoverished because he is a fool," commented her grandfather. When she would have protested, he held up one hand to stop her and added, "A charming fool, I grant you, but he is young, and we must all hope that he will improve with age."

Satisfied with this opinion, which marched so closely with her own, Elizabeth nodded. When he didn't prompt her, she returned to their original topic and said quietly, "I want someone who will not care only for what Society thinks. Someone who will care about helping other people more than the cut of his coat. You have taught me that much. A bit of kindness goes a long way in keeping one's household and estate happy and prosperous."

"Elizabeth, the men who have courted you are all young—not much older than Val. You give him the benefit of the doubt more often than you should. Why don't you see if you can do the same for the young men who would court you?"

She heaved a sigh, but said, "I will try, Grandfather, but it is not just that. I . . . I want a husband who is not afraid to be his own man, one who is not afraid of doing what is right, even if Society threatens to turn its back on him."

"And yet I think you would not wish to marry outside

your own class, outside of Society. Perhaps you are asking too much. Perhaps you might try to be a little less exacting and a little more forgiving." The earl put an arm around her shoulders, giving a little squeeze.

"You may be right. Very well, I will try to look for someone I can love, even if his armor is slightly tarnished."

"Good. That is all I ask. And if you never wed, my dear, at least you will be here to look after me when I do get old," he said with a wink. Rising, the earl pulled her to his feet and said, "It is time for tea, and I am famished. I received a letter from Avery this morning. I will share it with you and your grandmother."

"How is he? Fully recovered, I hope."

Rotherford nodded and said, "Yes, he is already itching to go back to Charleston. I think there must be a girl there."

"Avery? Surely not! If you think I am persnickety, you cannot possibly know Avery's views on girls. They must be goddesses in appearance, saints in deportment, and lively in conversation."

"A daunting combination, to be sure," he replied, taking her hand and heading back to the house.

"An impossible combination!" said Elizabeth.

"Your cousin is a harridan!"

"Steady on," said Lord Avery Winters, his initial reaction to this statement making him frown, an activity that made the tender wound on his forehead protest. "Blast," he muttered, stroking his brow.

"Sorry, Winters, but it has to be said."

"Does it? Because you offered for her, and she turned you down? Perhaps you just took her by surprise. Give it a day or two and then try again. You know she used to fancy you before you went off to war."

"Did she? Her rejection has made me forget all that, as I don't doubt she has already done."

"Your pride is only wounded."

"And so it should be! Everyone knew I was going to Wintersford to ask for her hand in marriage, and everyone will know that she rejected me! I tell you, Winters, Elizabeth has turned into a cold one. Why, she is positively an antidote. Someone should take her down a peg or two."

"Someone? You? Be careful, Wakefield. I would hate to have to call you out."

Sir Landon's hand went to his side, to the sword he had grown so accustomed to wearing during his years serving with Wellington. The sword was gone now, and he laughed.

"Nothing so rash as that, Winters, but something should be done to make her understand that she cannot treat a fellow so callously."

Avery grunted and said, "I cannot deny that Elizabeth's inability to settle on a husband has been trying for the family."

"Of course, it cannot please any of you. I don't understand why your grandfather has not put paid to the problem and chosen a husband for the hoyden."

Avery's eyes narrowed at this, but he said nothing. While he thought that his cousin's unmarried state was curious, he would not go so far as to agree with his friend. He commended his grandfather's tolerance in allowing Elizabeth to choose her own husband.

At the same time, he had assumed she would accept Wakefield. It annoyed him that she would reject his oldest friend. Perhaps he would have a talk with the silly girl. For one thing, Wakefield could be a dangerous enemy. He let his temper rule his actions, and Avery feared that he would find a way to pay back Elizabeth for his humiliation.

Just another reason for him to suggest strongly that she find a husband and wed as soon as possible.

In the hall, he heard a knock on the door. A moment

later, his manservant entered the small parlor with an envelope on a silver salver.

Reading it made Avery grimace, but he said, "Get my hat and coat, Grimes. Sorry, Wakefield. I can't commiserate with you any longer. I have been summoned to Rotherford House."

"Perhaps your grandfather has finally come to his senses and is forcing your cousin to wed," said Sir Landon.

"No, it is my grandmother and mother who have summoned me. They want to make sure I really am still kicking."

"There you are, dear boy! I could not rest until I had seen you," said his mother. Avery crossed the plush green carpet and placed a kiss on the cheeks of both his mother and grandmother. To Lady Louisa, he bowed and kissed the back of her hand before taking the single chair across from the sofa where the three ladies perched.

Smiling, he asked, "I do hope my appearance meets with your approval, ladies."

"Indeed it does," said Lady Louisa.

His mother smiled and his grandmother, the formidable Countess Rotherford, nodded regally.

"Does your wound trouble you much?" asked his mother.

"No, it is healing nicely, Mother." Feeling rather ill at ease, despite the comfortable chair, Winters asked, "Was there some other reason for my summons?"

"Yes, my boy," said his grandmother.

With a glance at Lady Louisa, his cousin Elizabeth's maternal grandmother, Avery said, "I assume it has something to do with Elizabeth's slapdash rejection of Sir Landon."

"Such a clever puss," chortled Lady Louisa, who had always treated him like one of her own brood.

"Pray do not be impertinent, Avery," said the countess, looking at him through her lorgnette. "Elizabeth has every right to reject Sir Landon."

"And that is why you have called me here? To tell me that you are overjoyed that Elizabeth has yet another rejection under her belt? How many were there while I was away, by the by?"

"Now you *are* being impertinent," said his mother.

The countess put a hand on her daughter-in-law's arm to silence her. "We will not discuss numbers, Avery. Rather, we are here to see if we can come up with someone who might . . . succeed where others have failed."

"A very good thing it would be," muttered Avery.

"And what is that supposed to mean?"

"It means, Grandmother, that Sir Landon is not going to accept his fate quietly. He is talking about making Elizabeth the talk of the town, and I do not wish to be put in the position of having to call out my friend to defend my cousin's honor."

His mother gasped, but his grandmother said, "Poppycock! It should not come to that. Besides, what business is it of Landon Wakefield if our Elizabeth decides not to marry—him or anyone else, for that matter?"

Lady Louisa tapped her friend's arm and said, "But it is Elizabeth's marriage we wish to arrange."

The countess grunted but remained silent, giving Lady Louisa the opportunity to speak. "We want you to help us locate someone whom Elizabeth might fancy. I fear we were all lulled into a sense of security, thinking she would accept Sir Landon when he returned. He was not very prompt in presenting himself, however, and that annoyed her—to say the least."

"So you are saying she was merely mad at him and might reconsider if he should press his suit?"

Lady Louisa colored up and shook her head. "No, I don't think so. Not considering the things she had to say about the young man. No, we must think of someone new, someone fresh."

"Someone she doesn't know too much about," said his grandmother. "Rotherford and I have discussed it. From his chat with her, we know that the girl has some odd notions, to be sure, but given the right man, without too much time to think about it, she will make it to the altar."

"And you expect me to come up with someone?" asked Avery.

"We only want you to put some thought into it, Avery dear. I mean, the Season is almost upon us."

"I had planned to return to Charleston . . ."

"After the Season will be soon enough, don't you think?" said his grandmother.

Viscount Winters looked from one face to the other—from his mother's hopeful expression to Lady Louisa's pleading one, and finally to his grandmother's commanding face. What could he say?

"Very well, I will do my best."

"That is all we ask, my boy," said his grandmother. "I need not tell you that it is Elizabeth's happiness that we wish to secure."

Lord Winters scoffed and said, "That, and a man who is handsome enough, rich enough, and foolish enough to ask for the hand of the most elusive Lady Elizabeth Winters!"

Avery settled into the hackney cab and gave the driver directions. How the devil was he going to find someone his cousin didn't already know? It was not as if the Season would bring that many new faces. A few fellows up from the country, but like as not Elizabeth, in her eight years on the town, had already met them and probably rejected most of them. There were others, like Sir Landon, who had finally sold out after the long fight against

Bonaparte, but he was not at all certain any of them were suitable. He sighed, putting the problem from his mind.

First, he needed to find his Good Samaritan, Captain Sparks, and thank him one last time. If the man had not sought him out, Avery would most certainly have perished when the ship went down.

Avery flicked open the curtains to watch the passing grand houses change to more modest ones and then gradually to the less savory part of London—the docks. He had made inquiries and discovered where Captain Sparks was staying.

He had planned to make arrangements with the captain to return to the United States. It would have to be postponed now, of course, but he needed to thank the captain again.

Avery let his mind drift back to Charleston. While taking care of the family business there, he had met Miss Thurgood—Millie, she had told him he might call her. Her golden hair and blue eyes haunted his dreams. Now, since his brush with death, he felt the need to get on with his life, and he rather thought Millie should be a part of it.

Whistling jauntily, Avery entered the Hanged Goose, a tavern inn. It was clean and neat, unlike most of its neighbors, but it was still dark and gloomy within. He shut the door and waited for his eyes to adjust. The landlord, seeing his fine clothes, hurried forth to bow and scrape.

"Good evening, m'lord. What can I bring you?"

"Brandy, your best." Avery spotted the captain in the corner and added, "Two glasses, if you please."

"Very good, m'lord."

Avery crossed to the far corner and waited for the captain to look up. The eyes that met his were clouded with drink, but the captain recognized him and sat up, shoving the other chair out for him to sit.

"Evening, Winters. What brings you to this fine establishment?"

Judging from the almost empty bottle of gin on the table, Avery was surprised the captain could make sense. Sitting down, he replied, "I was looking for you, Captain Sparks. I am leaving London and wanted to thank you again for saving my life."

The landlord arrived with the glasses and the bottle. Avery busied himself pouring a generous portion into the glasses before lifting his glass and adding, "To your very good health and good fortune, Captain."

Gideon Sparks watched the amber liquid disappear from his glass before picking up the other one. His voice was gravelly as he said, "And to yours, Winters."

He drained it and set it on the table. Avery filled it again, splashing a bit into his own glass, too.

"I also wanted to find out when you will be returning to the United States."

"Not any time soon," grumbled the captain.

"Really? Then if your plans should happen to march with mine, I would be pleased to book passage on your ship."

The captain drained his glass again. This time he picked up the bottle and filled it himself. He held it up in question, but Avery shook his head.

"Then you must not be in any hurry to return to my country," said the captain.

"On the contrary, but I have obligations to take care of here in England. In two or three months' time . . . My family's businesses there could use a firm hand, and . . . well, there is another reason, a more personal reason I would like to return to Charleston. So, when do you sail?"

"When hell freezes over, I believe the saying goes."

Avery frowned. "You wish to remain in England?"

The captain laughed, though the sound held little enjoyment.

Avery stiffened and said, "Have I said something amusing?"

"Not at all, Lord Winters. There is not a drop of amusement in what you said."

"Then I don't understand . . ."

Gideon Sparks's eyes blazed in anger. With a curse, he threw the glass across the room, where it shattered against the wall.

"How do you propose that I should sail back to the United States, Lord Winters? On what vessel? The last I looked, mine was resting on the floor of the ocean. That makes it rather difficult to sail in."

Avery didn't respond immediately. Instead, he sat back, lost in his own thoughts. The captain filled his empty gin glass with brandy and drank it down. He poured another, but this one he simply cupped in his large hands, swirling the contents.

"You see this little whirlpool," he said finally, holding up the glass to show Avery the small funnel the swirling liquid had formed. "That is a symbol of my career as a captain, swirling ever downward. I was once considered a fair-haired sailor—one who could not set a foot wrong. Decorated in battle at the age of six and twenty, a captain by seven and twenty. Having served my country, I had two ships of my own before I turned thirty."

"An illustrious career," said Avery. "One loss should not . . ."

"Two."

"Two?"

"I lost my larger ship last year. A damned freakish storm. Winds of hurricane force—no more than six minutes it took. It shouldn't have gone down, but it did. And now this. Another storm, but one I would have been able to ride out. Then that blasted ship came out of nowhere and . . . damned bad luck. Where the devil did he come from?" With a string of expletives, he emptied the glass.

"I am sorry," said Avery.

The captain waved his hand in dismissal and said, "History, that is all it amounts to now, just history. So tell me, Winters, what have you been doing since we arrived in London?"

"Seeing friends, visiting my, uh, tailor," Avery added, looking at the captain's dirty shirt and unkempt appearance.

"Just as any fine gentleman should. I, on the other hand, have been looking for a position. First as captain, then as first mate. No one will have me. Sailors are a superstitious lot, you see, and with my history, I am considered something of a Jonah. No one wants a Jonah on board—not as a captain, certainly, nor even as the lowest sailor."

"So you are saying you are ruined."

"You're a clever one, my fine friend."

Avery grimaced at this, but he was not done. "Perhaps there might be something I can do."

The captain drew himself up, looked down his nose at Avery, and said distinctly, "I do not accept charity."

"Nor do I offer it."

"Good," said the captain, slumping in his chair again.

"Why don't you come to my club for dinner tomorrow night? Perhaps we may be able to come up with some plan—a plan of mutual benefit."

The captain slumped further in his chair and shook his head. "It cannot hurt to listen."

Avery pulled out a pencil and a calling card and scribbled the address of his club on the back. "Eight o'clock. At the very least, we'll share a decent meal and another bottle. It's the least I can do for the man who saved my life."

As Avery left the tavern and entered the hackney cab, a plan began to form. His grandmother wanted a suitor for Elizabeth, someone new and different. He smiled. The captain fit both requirements. What was more, he was a desperate man.

Not, he amended, that a man would have to be desperate to pursue his cousin. Elizabeth was a beauty, and even if she was a little too exacting in her choice of husbands, she was also an heiress, and that went far in excusing her fussiness.

Avery debated for a moment whether he could justify introducing her to a man who was merely after her fortune, but the answer was yes. Elizabeth would be settled, and he could return to Charleston and Millie knowing that his grandmother had been appeased. Everyone would be happy!

Elizabeth rose from her bed with a groan. How many nights had it been since she slept? No, she corrected herself, since she went to sleep without hours of tossing and turning. Eight or ten, surely—since Sir Landon had offered for her and been summarily rejected.

She strolled to the window and threw back the yellow brocade curtain to gaze at the full moon. She needn't have been so tacky, so blunt. It was ever the same for her. She never knew when to let things pass by unsaid. An unruly tongue, her governesses had said, wagging a finger at her.

Elizabeth's chin jutted out, and her eyes narrowed as she remembered her conversation with Landon—for that was how she still thought of him—ever the daring, handsome boy who had charmed his way into her young heart.

They had been children together, for heaven's sake! Surely he expected plain speaking from her!

Elizabeth's weary eyes closed, and she sucked in a deep breath of air. When she had received word that he would be coming home, her heart had soared. She had envisioned his entrance into the study: His hair in disarray, his clothes—no, his uniform—mussed from hours in the saddle, hurrying to her side.

And almost three months after his return, what had she received instead? A fine dandy of a man, dressed in the latest fashion, his hair carefully arranged to look windswept, probably come from the arms of his latest conquest.

What a fool she had been! Had he not thought she would hear of his reckless behavior since returning to England? Or did he simply not care?

Obviously, he had not cared enough about her to come to her immediately. She had wondered if he had missed her the way she was missing him. That kiss they had shared the night before he left, six long years ago—it had meant nothing to him.

Elizabeth shrugged the heartbreak off her shoulders. She was no longer angry, but she still had to work on not being disappointed. The life she had imagined for herself was not to be. Now was not the time for despair. Now was the time to marshal her forces and find someone new who would cherish her and love her, a man she could love and respect in return.

Respect. That was the rub. Where, amongst all the fribbles and Corinthians, was she going to find a man of her station who could earn her respect? As far as she could tell, without respect, there could be no love.

With a moan, Elizabeth returned to her bed, arranged the covers, and resumed her quest for sleep.

Chapter Two

"Welcome to Boodle's, sir. May I direct you to someone?"

"Lord Winters asked me to come by," said Gideon, his eyes straying from the man in fine livery to the room beyond.

"I believe his lordship is in the dining room, Mr.—"

"Captain Sparks."

"Yes, of course. He did say you would be coming. Henson will take you in," said the servant, accepting Gideon's greatcoat and hat.

He crossed the soft carpets, following the footman until they arrived at a large dining room. Many of the members were already having their dinner, and they spared him only a cursory glance.

"Captain, welcome to Boodle's. I'm so glad you could come," said the viscount, rising slightly.

Gideon took the chair opposite Lord Winters.

"A glass of burgundy?"

"Yes, thank you." He watched the ruby liquid fill the glass and tasted it before sitting back. "Nice place."

"Yes, a good place to meet friends when one doesn't have a huge home to do so. I could use Rotherford House, but I never know when either my mother or grandmother is going to take it into her head to come to town. One of the drawbacks to having the family estate a mere day and a half from London."

"I wouldn't know. There was not an estate in my family. I am where I am by the sweat of my own brow."

Gideon knew his tone bordered on belligerent, but he could not keep his pride in check. It had suffered too many blows in the past year, and he would be damned if he were going to allow an English popinjay to look down his aristocratic nose at him. He had not forgotten the war.

Avery was studying him thoughtfully, and Gideon's color deepened beneath his weathered face and reddish beard.

"Sorry, I am not usually so churlish," he grumbled.

"No, no, think nothing of it. In your circumstances, I would probably throw up my hands and give in," said Winters.

Gideon caught the laughter in his host's eyes and shook his head. "You're an impudent fellow."

"Every chance I get. However, I do not mean to belittle your concerns. I mean, I choose to work in my family's businesses, so I do have a more realistic view of what it takes to succeed in life through hard work. The fact that, should I fail, my situation will not change gravely, does not prevent me from seeing what is at stake for others. Sorry, I rather sound like my all-seeing grandfather—a proper bore that can be, I assure you. And the fact that he is always right does not lessen the impact."

"I knew when I met you in Charleston that you were not merely a man of business—despite the fact that you didn't use your title when you booked passage. It doesn't alter my opinion of you. Now, you said you had something in mind that might benefit both of us."

"Of course, but let's have dinner before we get into that."

The servants arrived with the first course, stewed trout and pea soup. Gideon was surprised at how good the food tasted, but then, he had not eaten since early that morning, when he had sought out an old friend to inquire about a position. His appetite had fled when Ames informed him that he didn't have a need for his services.

His practical side took over, and Gideon set upon the meal with great gusto. After the second course of braised pheasant and lamb cutlets with several accompanying dishes, Gideon looked up to find his host still watching him. Suddenly, he felt like an insect caught in a spider's web.

Putting down his fork and knife, he said, "Are you ready to tell me what you have in mind for me now? You said something about a plan to our mutual benefit."

"Yes, yes, but I haven't worked it all out yet. What I really would like is for you to come down to Wintersford for a visit. I want you to meet my grandfather."

Gideon's eyes narrowed. "He's the one whose business you were attending to in Charleston?"

"The very same."

"I don't much like the idea of playing cat and mouse. You tell me right now what you have in mind, and maybe I'll come along."

Lord Winters chuckled at this, but he nodded. "I really don't know for certain. I know we have some business with shipping, but we don't actually have a fleet of brigantines, so I am not certain where you might fit in."

"I told you I won't accept charity, and that includes someone making up a job for me where there really isn't one."

Gideon's dark eyes were fixed on his host, ready to detect any sign of duplicity. He had only accepted charity once as a young man. Too late had he recognized the gift had been nothing but a manipulative woman's trap. He would not make that mistake again, no matter how desperate his situation might be. He had pulled himself up by the bootstraps once; he could do it again.

"Good. Then you will appreciate the fact that I am not making any promises. If my grandfather or his secretary think there is a legitimate spot for you in one of our affairs, then they will let us both know. In the meanwhile, you can see a bit of the countryside. My grandmother may be a regular tartar, but I think you will be able to hold your own against her," said Avery, smiling slightly as he added, "Or anyone else, for that matter. What do you say?"

Gideon picked up the glass of wine and said, "I say thank you for your kind invitation, Winters. When do you wish to leave?"

Gideon steadied himself against the building before resuming his walk back to the inn. He was befuddled, but he was hardly drunk. It would take more than an English lord to outdrink him—a good thing, too. He had things to do before his journey the next morning.

He stumbled and shook his head. Perhaps he had taken one glass too many. At least he had not lost his tiny store of coins. Instead, he had added to them, playing cards with the viscount for small stakes. Still, at this rate, it would take years to win enough to purchase another ship.

"Wot 'ave we 'ere, Robbie? A fine captain, it seems."

"A very fine cap'ain," said the other man, taking hold of Gideon's sleeve.

Gideon grinned like an idiot and grabbed the man's coat. "Got any gin?" he asked, breathing into the pock-marked face.

"Gin? We got somethin' better for you, me fine cap'ain," said the man.

Gideon felt something hard against his side while the other man's hand went for his purse.

"Better than this?" said Gideon, his elbow sending the gunman sprawling while he bobbed his head forward, connecting against the other assailant's nose with a satisfying crack. Holding his nose, the man screamed and doubled over. Gideon's knee came up, catching the man's chin and sending him flying. The first man staggered to his feet, cursing loudly as he flung himself on Gideon.

Gideon grabbed the man's head and gave it a twist, throwing him back to the ground. He placed a boot on the man's throat and smiled.

"Want more?"

"No! No!"

"Then give me what's in your pockets and be quick about it!"

"But you can't . . . all right, all right! It's all I've got! I swear, Cap'ain."

"What about your friend? Check his pockets."

The man scrambled across the ground and emptied his accomplice's pockets. He held out a gold watch. Gideon snapped his fingers and caught it easily.

"Wot now, Cap'ain?" said the man, his weaselly eyes shifting back and forth.

"Where do you live?"

"'Ere 'bouts."

"If I want to talk to you sometime, to, ah, secure your services, where might you be located?"

"You kin allus ask fer me, Guinny, or Robbie there, at th' Black Vine."

"Very well. Now, get out of here and take him with you."

"Thank you, Cap'ain, that's very generous o' you, Cap'ain."

Gideon picked up the rusty pistol and put it in his pocket along with the gold watch and the meager stash of coins. It was good to know that he could still hold his own in a fight. And if some people would be shocked that he had stolen the thieves' money, he didn't really care. He was too poor to care.

Whistling, Gideon returned to his room and stripped off his clothes. He poured some water from the pitcher into the washbasin and scrubbed himself from head to foot. Throwing this water out, he proceeded to wash all of his clothes and lay them out before the fire—a small task considering that he had purchased only one shirt since arriving with just the clothes on his back.

He eyed his coat and shook his head. He had said he would not accept charity, but he would have felt much more comfortable about visiting such a wealthy estate if he had at least one more change of clothes.

Gideon removed his purse and counted out the coins, adding the few he had taken off his would-be robbers. Enough to buy another pair of pants. He grimaced. He was not a vain man, but he had always prided himself on being well-groomed. Perhaps it came from growing up with nothing.

He glanced up to search his face in the cracked mirror behind the dressing table. They would just have to take him as he was. There was nothing he could do about it now.

Picking up a brush, he cleaned his coat and overcoat as best he could. Then he stretched out on the narrow bed and slept—his dreams coming to him on waves like the ocean he loved so very much.

Gideon tried to fix a casual expression on his face, but the façade of the Winters' country home threatened to overwhelm him. It was made of carved limestone and seemed to go on forever. He had seen many large houses, but this one he would classify as a castle if it were made of gray stone.

How the devil could a fellow ever feel at ease in such a place? He stole a glance at his traveling companion, whose whip touched the leader's flank as they circled around the wide drive and stopped at the front door.

Gideon jumped down from the curricle and watched as four footmen hurried toward the carriage, opening the boot and taking out the bags. A groom appeared from nowhere and took charge of the equipage.

"Welcome to my humble abode," said Lord Winters. "By

the way, you mustn't let anything my grandmother says unnerve you. She will say the most outrageous things and then expect everyone to pretend that they are everyday commonplaces. Most startling, I assure you. But then, I suspect that is the very purpose. Come along."

Gideon fell into step beside his host.

"Oh, and one other thing. I think it would be better if everyone thought we were friends, not just chance acquaintances because I happened to book passage on your ship. You don't mind, do you?"

"I suppose not. Do you mean that you are not allowed to bring strangers to stay?"

"I can bring anyone I please, but for our purposes, I think our being friends would look less strange. Besides, we have shared a number of meals, both on board the ship and then at my club last night. That makes us friends."

"If it makes you feel any better, we can say we have been friends forever," said Gideon. He thought he would never understand the aristocracy.

"Hello, Finch. How are you?"

The ancient butler smiled slightly as his young master helped him rise from his bow. "I am very well, Master Avery, m'lord."

"I am delighted to hear it." The old man dusted away a tear, and Lord Winters said, "Now, now. None of that. I'm home now. No need to fret. And see, I have brought Captain Sparks, the man who saved my life. Without him, I would not have made it through the mishap."

"We are eternally grateful to you, Captain. Welcome to Wintersford."

"Thank you. Finch, is it?" Gideon took the gnarled fingers and gave his hand a shake.

The servant sputtered in surprise and said, "Yes, Captain. Your rooms are ready, Master Avery. We have put the captain in the room next to yours."

"Capital. That way, we can help each other to our rooms

at night when we are jug-bitten." Avery chuckled at the butler's sigh. "We'll see ourselves upstairs, Finch."

"Very good, m'lord."

As they mounted the first set of stairs, Avery whispered, "Finch is a Methodist at heart—very starchy. He doesn't approve of excess in anything, especially drink."

"Then why would you bait him?" asked Gideon, giving his new friend a hard look.

"He expects it. When I don't tease him, he begins to think that something is the matter. When I was sixteen, he told my grandfather he thought I might be hiding something terrible because I had been on such good behavior. Little did he know, I was sneaking out every night and sleeping with the local tavern girl. My good behavior was just a ruse to cover up my indiscretions. Since then, I make sure old Finch has something to worry about."

"What a complicated life you lead," murmured Gideon.

While Avery continued down the hall, Gideon paused by a portrait of a girl mounted on a large horse. Her eyes were dancing with laughter, as if someone had just told her a riddle. Her expression made him smile. He caught up with his host.

"This is my room," Avery was saying. "You are next to me. We keep country hours here, so supper will be at six o'clock. I'll knock on your door. If there is one thing my grandfather insists upon, it is punctuality."

Entering his own room, Gideon said, "I will be ready."

Gideon surveyed his quarters with a smile. He might not have grown up in luxury, but since becoming a captain with two ships, he had experienced how the other half lived. He strolled across the room and looked out the window at the wide lawn with the elaborate stable beyond. Judging from this estate, the Earl of Rotherford lived better than more than half the rest of the population.

Fingering the rich velvet brocade of the drapes, Gideon shook his head. Everything about the chamber spelled quality, from the draperies to the marble fireplace to the heavy walnut furniture.

Gideon smiled and sat down on the small settee in front of the fire to remove his boots. There was a knock on the door and a fussy little man with wispy gray hair sailed into the room. He carried a stack of white linen, which he deposited on the bed before turning to stare at Gideon, lips pursed and hands on hips.

"Forgive me for intruding, Captain," he lisped. "Lord Winters thought you might have need of my services."

"And you are?"

"Oh, silly me. I am Grimes, Lord Winters' personal servant. If you will permit me," he said, crossing over to Gideon and studying him intensely. With a "tsk, tsk," he said, "The beard really must go, Captain. While facial hair was once almost obligatory, it is now terribly démodé."

"It keeps my face warm at sea. I'll keep it."

"Oh, I . . . I didn't think about that. Well, perhaps . . . if you wouldn't mind rising?"

A bemused Gideon rose, and the valet had to throw his head back to see his face. "My, my, so very tall. At least half a head taller than Lord Winters. I'm not at all certain these things will do." With a sigh, the valet crossed back to the bed and picked up a shirt from the pile he had deposited there. "Might as well try it on. I shall have to tell Sukey how much to let them out."

"I don't need any shirts," protested Gideon, stepping away from the fussy little man.

"I beg to differ, sir. Perhaps you have other belongings, but the footman who unpacked your clothing confirmed that you do need shirts."

"I am not some charity case," growled Gideon.

"Of course not, Captain, and I am offended that you would think we viewed you as such. You must know that all of us, from the lowest potboy to Mr. Finch himself, we are all aware of the sacrifice you made to save our good Master Avery. Why, some gentlemen would have gone back for their belongings rather than a passenger, but you didn't, sir, and we are all most grateful. So you see, since your lack of suitable garments is due to your act of heroism, we are only too happy to be able to repay you, however modestly, by seeing to it that you are properly clothed."

Gideon smiled at the little man whose chest had swelled with pride as he delivered his speech. Given the manservant's vehemence, he would feel a cad to turn him down.

Gideon removed his shirt and said, "Very well, Grimes, we will proceed."

That being said, he allowed the servant to place the shirt over his head. When he put his arms down, there was an ominous rip.

"Tsk, tsk. Much too small. I was afraid of that. Very well, I have another. One of the earl's shirts, when he was less . . . robust. At least the sleeves will be long enough."

This garment proved too large, but Grimes assured him that it would take the mysterious Sukey only a stitch or two to alter it perfectly.

Having made this concession, Gideon was then pushed and prodded into other garments. He was about to lose his temper when the valet announced that they were finished.

"You will have to make do with your own things for tonight, Captain, but by tomorrow night . . ." He kissed his fingertips and sashayed to the door. "Will there be anything else?"

"Not now. Thank you, Grimes."

"You are most welcome, Captain."

And then Gideon was alone. He took out his watch and checked the time. Almost six o'clock. He glanced at the mirror and ran a hand through his thick brown curls. His hand lingered on the beard. He had worn one for so long, he could not imagine going without it. Still, perhaps it was time for a change.

He glanced at his image and grinned. He was as ready

for this dinner as he would ever be. He supposed he would meet the earl tonight—the man who could help him get his life back, if he was favorably impressed.

Gideon ignored the twinge of tightness this brought to his shoulders and strolled out of the room. At the end of the hall, he paused to study the paintings that lined the wall. Most were from other times, when the men wore ruffles and powdered wigs. Again he stopped in front of the portrait of the young lady on horseback.

What a beauty! And such spirit in those eyes—those deep green eyes. She was petite, almost childlike in stature on the horse's back. Of course, painters did not necessarily take proportion into account when they rendered their subjects on canvas. Surely such a small lady would never be mounted on such a powerful steed.

He looked into those eyes again. They seemed to be laughing at him. Gideon shook himself. Idleness was making him fancy something that was not there. Still, she was quite beautiful. Her habit had a timeless quality about it, and he found it impossible to guess from which era she was.

"There you are," called Lord Winters. "I knocked, but you didn't answer. Are you as hungry as I am? Let's go down to the drawing room and have a glass of wine before dinner. I will introduce you to the family."

Gideon turned away from the portrait and said, "Who is that girl?"

"Oh, just some relation. Did you find your room comfortable?"

"Yes, and thank you for sending your valet."

Avery chuckled and said, "I know. He is terribly fidgety, but he means well, and when I mentioned that your wardrobe had gone down with the ship, well, he was delighted to have some way to repay you."

"For my heroism," said Gideon with a self-deprecating chuckle. "I don't suppose I should tell him that any self-respecting sea captain would make certain everyone was safe before he abandoned his ship."

"No, no, it is much better this way. Now, let me warn you again about my grandmother. She is accustomed to getting her own way and her manner of speech is, shall we say, very direct."

"And when one returns the favor?" asked Gideon.

Avery paused and turned to stare at him. With only a hint of amusement in his voice, he said, "I don't recall anyone ever doing so, except perhaps my grandfather. He is not a meek sort, just much more rational than Grandmother."

"And will there be other family members?" asked Gideon as they continued down the wide staircase.

"My mother is here, I know. She has a very sweet disposition. And I think my widowed neighbor, Lady Louisa Upton, will be here. She usually is. She is my grandmother's best friend, but they are as different as night and day. That's all, I'm afraid. And here we are," he announced as the footman opened the door to the drawing room.

"Avery, darling, it is so good to see you again," said his mother, rising from her chair and coming forward to receive her son's embrace and a kiss on her cheek. "And this must be the good Captain Sparks."

"Indeed it is, Mother. Captain Gideon Sparks, the man who saved my life. Captain, this is my mother, Lady Winters."

Gideon sketched a bow and smiled down at the faded beauty. Her gown was red but it was shot through with silver, just like her hair. When she smiled at him, he could easily see the resemblance to her son.

"I am delighted to meet you, Captain. I cannot tell you what a great debt of gratitude I feel toward you."

"There is no need, madam. I would have been derelict in my duty had I not made sure your son was safe."

"Oh, of course," she said, taking his arm. With an elegant sweep of her short train, she turned and led him to the others. "Allow me to introduce you to everyone."

On the sofa was a woman with steel gray hair. As they approached, she lifted her lorgnette to inspect him like a piece of livestock she might wish to purchase. This brought a smile to his eyes as Gideon bowed before her. When he looked up, one brow had risen considerably and the lorgnette was lowered very slowly. If she was trying to depress his pretensions, he thought, she would have to do better than that. She was not the first woman to look at him askance. He was glad, however, that he had cleaned up. Otherwise, he would think her curled lip and upturned nose were due to his poor hygiene.

"This is my mother-in-law, Lady Rotherford, the Countess of Rotherford," said Lady Winters.

"How do you do, madam?" said Gideon, the laughter in his eyes threatening to spill forth from his lips.

"I would do better, my good man, if you would address me correctly. I am Lady Rotherford."

A small chuckle escaped his lips, and her eyes ignited with fire. He shook his head and said, "Madam, if I knew how to do that, I would be happy to, but since I don't know, I thought I would err on the side of caution. We don't have titles where I come from."

"Do you mean that you do not know the proper etiquette for addressing a lady?"

This came from the lady beside the arrogant countess, and Gideon turned to her with a relieved smile. She turned a delicate pink and waved her painted fan before her face. Her eyes, he noticed immediately, were the same color as those of the girl in the painting. Could this round little woman have been that beautiful girl?

"In my business dealings, I have run into a few lords, madam, but I am not accustomed to dealing with ladies—ladies such as you," he added, bowing over her hand.

With a giggle, she said, "I am Lady Upton, though most people call me Lady Louisa, since I grew up with that title. Cordelia, here, as she told you, is Lady Rotherford. You might address her as countess, but that sounds a little . . . casual. You may address any of us—myself, Lady Winters, or Lady Rotherford—as 'my lady'."

"Thank you, Lady Louisa. It is kind of you to instruct this provincial rustic."

"I would not call you rustic, Captain," she said.

"Ah, another kindness." He turned back to his hostess and said, "Nice to make your acquaintance, Lady Rotherford."

Her lips were pursed in disapproval, but she nodded.

Lady Winters took his arm again and turned him to the other gentleman in the room. He was almost as tall as Gideon was, and his build was lean and hard for a man of some sixty years. He extended his hand and gave Gideon's hand a firm shake.

"Rotherford, Captain. Just call me Rotherford."

"Thank you, sir," he replied.

"Avery, come here and give me a kiss," demanded his grandmother, Lady Rotherford.

Avery did as he was bid and leaned over to give Lady Louisa a kiss, too. He shook his grandfather's hand and was pulled into a quick embrace.

"It's good to have you home and safe, son," said the older man.

"Thank you, Grandfather. It is good to be home, though I did enjoy myself immensely in Charleston. There are a few things I would like to introduce to our . . ."

"Not tonight. We will talk business later," said the earl with a nod to his wife. Turning back to Gideon, he asked, "What will you have to drink, Captain? The ladies are having wine—it's a very good French Bordeaux—but you can have something stronger, if you prefer. Whiskey?"

"That will be fine, sir."

The earl filled two glasses and offered them to the younger men. Then he raised his own glass and said, "To Captain Sparks!"

"Hear! Hear!" said Avery, smiling at the captain over the rim of his glass. "To life!"

Gideon drank to this one. He welcomed the warmth of the liquor as it went down. He was not accustomed to families, especially affluent English families. He was more used to self-made men, a few planter's sons, and scoundrels.

It was obvious that this was a close family. They were genuinely happy to see the viscount alive and whole. Gideon, who had never known the pleasure of having a family, found this oddly touching.

The butler announced dinner, and Gideon was surprised to find Lady Winters waiting for him to lead her through to the dining room. Dining hall would have been a more appropriate appellation for the room, he thought as he entered. It was long and wide, and paneled in a dark wood. Suits of armor graced each corner, and from the ceiling hung an enormous chandelier with countless candles. At least the table had been shortened to a reasonable length. It was set with a beautiful service of gold and silver that glittered in the candlelight.

Gideon was seated between the countess, who was at the end of the table, and Lady Winters. Opposite him was Winters, and beside the viscount was the smiling Lady Louisa. The earl sat at the other end of the table, opposite his wife.

As soon as they were seated, three servants carrying large silver trays entered the room through a door that was hidden in the paneling. The scent of food made his stomach rumble. The countess's nose went up another inch.

What a stuffy old dame she is! Well, it doesn't matter, he thought. *I will conclude my business with her husband and be away from here in a day or two.*

Lady Louisa made a contented sigh when the mulligatawny soup was placed in front of her. She smiled across the table and said, "My favorite. Tell me, Captain, have you spent much time here in England?"

"No, I . . ."

"Louisa, really, must you talk across the table?" interrupted the countess.

"Oh, for heaven's sake, Cordelia! It is not as if we are at a state dinner. With only the six of us, surely we can converse across the table."

"A splendid idea," said the earl. "How clever of our Louisa to have thought of it."

He raised his glass and fixed his wife with a challenging stare. After a second, she picked up her own glass, gave a regal nod, and drank.

Then she turned to Gideon and asked, "So, Captain Sparks, have you spent much time here in England?"

"No, Lady Rotherford, hardly any at all. My business keeps me very busy, and in the past, when my travels have brought me to England, I generally return home rather quickly."

"I suppose your wife must miss you very much," chimed in Lady Winters.

"I am not married, Lady Winters."

"What a shame," said Lady Louisa, her green eyes twinkling as she smiled at the countess.

Gideon frowned. Something was going on that he didn't know about. He glanced at the earl, who put down his spoon and pushed the bowl away. So he was not in on whatever was going on. Lord Winters, however, was giving his mother a speaking glance.

Again, Gideon reflected that whatever was going on didn't really concern him. He would be gone as soon as he had a chance to speak to the earl about a new ship. Surely the life of his grandson was worth a new ship.

The servants began gathering the bowls and plates and soon returned with the second removes—roasted duck in an orange sauce, boiled potatoes with tiny onions, and asparagus tips with some sort of white sauce.

Gideon forgot the little intrigues going on about him as he devoured the excellent repast.

When his plate was empty, and the footman came to claim it, he said, "Do you have any more of that bird? It was very good."

The startled footman looked to the butler, who in turn looked at his mistress. With a slight nod from her, the duck was once again produced and his plate filled.

From across the table, Lady Louisa Upton said, "It does my heart good to see a man enjoy his food. The late Lord Upton had a glorious appetite. Why, he could eat for absolutely hours and hours."

"Martin did love his food," said the earl, reaching across and patting Lady Louisa's hand in a brotherly fashion.

"I understand you are neighbors," said Gideon, trying for some innocuous comment. It occurred to him that he had been eating much more than he had been conversing. The others, he noticed, were sitting and sipping their wine while he finished.

"Yes, when Cordelia wed Rotherford, I wed my late husband, whose estate marches with Wintersford. I live in the dower house now that my nephew has inherited the estate."

"I see," said Gideon. He didn't really see. He was not certain exactly how these inheritances worked.

"Upton is a fine man, but he has a wife, and I didn't want to get in the way, so I moved to the dower house."

Winters grinned and said, "Lest you feel too overcome with sympathy for Lady Louisa, Captain, I should tell you that the dower house boasts some fifteen rooms and one of the loveliest gardens in this part of England."

"How kind of you to say so, Avery," said Lady Louisa. She smiled at Gideon and said, "I do love my flowers. I cannot wait to see what the newest ones will look like. I have friends who send me seeds and seedlings from all over the world. Every spring is a revelation."

"Before I leave, you will have to give me your direction, Lady Louisa. My travels frequently take me to South America, where I believe there are some very unusual species. I would be happy to send some to you."

"Would you?" she asked, her green eyes sparkling. At that moment, Gideon thought that the girl in the picture probably was a young Lady Louisa.

"I would be happy to do so," he said.

"What a fascinating life you must lead," said Lady Winters. "Traveling all over the world!"

"Do you not get homesick?" demanded the countess.

He turned and was met by that lorgnette again. "Not really. I feel very at home on board one of my ships."

"So you have more than one?" asked the earl.

"Well, no, sir. I have met with a series of misfortunes."

Lady Winters said, "And now you have no boats at all." She smiled at him and said, "Avery told me. How sad for you."

"Yes, it is."

Lady Rotherford said, "But tell me, Captain. Don't you wish to marry and have a family? A man must have children to carry on when he is gone. How can a man who is constantly at sea manage that? Surely a wife deserves as much."

Gideon turned to the countess. For once, he wished he had a quizzing glass. He had always thought them the most presumptuous accessories. Now, he would like to lift one and stare at the disagreeable woman. Instead, he took a deep breath and forced a smile.

"If I should ever marry, Lady Rotherford, I am certain my wife and I would arrive at a happy solution. Otherwise, we would never have to worry about children, would we?"

Across the table, Lady Louisa gasped and giggled. The countess, however, smiled at him for the first time and nodded.

Turning to her grandson, she said, "Your new friend speaks his mind. I like that in a man."

Gideon frowned at Lord Winters, but the man only raised his glass and said, "To men who speak their minds, and women who enjoy it."

Gideon sipped the ruby liquid while peering over the rim of the glass at his host and hostess. Evidently, he had passed some strange test, because conversation became more general and relaxed. He was surprised time had passed so quickly when the ladies rose to leave the gentlemen to their brandy and port.

The earl offered him a cigar. The footman hurried forward to light it.

Rotherford then turned to his grandson and asked, "So, Avery, my boy, what improvements did you have in mind for our properties over in the United States?"

The younger man looked at Gideon and winked. "Our agreement with the plantation owners to purchase their cotton exclusively was signed without any problem. Now all we have to do is make certain we find a way to ship it economically, and our profits should increase nicely. Our exports should do well—again, providing we can find an economical manner of transport."

The earl turned from his grandson to Gideon and said, "What do you plan to do now that you have lost both of your ships, sir?"

"I had hoped to sign on with another ship."

"You have not done so yet?"

"Not yet."

"Something to think about," murmured the older man. Then he rose and said, "I think we should join the ladies now. I have a feeling they are waiting on us. In the country, it is not often that we get such an interesting visitor as you, Captain."

"Thank you," said Gideon, also rising and following his host out of the room and down the wide corridor to the drawing room. When they entered, the ladies fell silent. A second later, all three started talking at once.

Yes, thought Gideon. *Something is definitely going on.*

Lady Rotherford asked, "Do you play cards, Captain?"

"Indeed I do, madam."

Her eyes glinted with interest, and she said, "Then come over here and play a hand of piquet with me."

Gideon never refused a challenge, and he soon found himself in a lively game for penny stakes. He played casually at first, allowing the countess to win.

"You do not play very well, Captain," she commented bluntly as she tallied the points. He looked up from shuffling the cards and smiled.

Half an hour later, he again looked up from the cards in his hands and smiled at his opponent. Lady Rotherford glared back.

Her eyes narrowed, and she snapped, "You have crumbs in that beard of yours."

He brushed the thick beard and said affably, "Thank you, ma'am."

"As I said before, Captain Sparks, the proper appellation is 'my lady,'" she said.

"I know you will forgive my lapses, my lady."

When this did not have the proper effect on him, she snapped, "Why do you wear that thing?"

"My beard? For one thing, it keeps my face warm when I am out to sea."

"You are not out to sea now," she said, playing her card with a flourish. "Nor are you likely to be, since you don't have a ship to captain."

He looked at the queen of hearts and seriously thought about not winning. Was it polite to allow one's hostess to win? With a quick glance around the sumptuously furnished drawing room, he played his ace and took the trick.

Her lips tightened, and she pitched her remaining cards onto the table. "Your game. Again."

"Thank you, my lady," he replied. He could swear he heard her grinding her teeth as she rose and left the table.

Gathering the small pile of coins and placing them in his coat pocket, Gideon stood up and strolled over to the window. Staring into the dark night, he shook his head. He didn't mind being on land in the daylight when he could see his surroundings. At night, however, without the rolling deck beneath his feet, he felt slightly off balance. How long would it be before he could go back to sea?

Gideon stroked his beard, a wicked grin on his lips. Perhaps he should shave it off. Few of the men he had met in London had beards. Not that he cared. He had never cared for what others did or thought.

From the hall, Gideon heard the case clock chiming the hour—ten o'clock. He wondered if he might be able to slip away to his room. He was unaccustomed to such close company with strangers, especially proper ladies such as these. He was more comfortable with a very different sort of lady.

Touching his sleeve, Lady Winters said, "You have wandered very far away, Captain."

He smiled down at her and shook his head. "Just thinking how out of place I feel here."

"Out of place? Oh, you mean you are usually at sea. Yes, I suppose this must be quite a change. Still, we are all so thankful to you for saving Avery, we are glad to have the chance to tell you so in person."

"I told you, Lady Winters . . ."

"Yes, I know you were only doing your duty, but since it was our Avery, we are still grateful. I am so sorry about your ship. Do you have any idea what you will do now?"

His jaw clenched and he shook his head. He wished everyone would quit asking him that. He had finally stopped asking himself.

His silence caused Lady Winters to say, "I am sorry. I shouldn't have said anything."

"No, it is all right. And to be honest, I am not certain what I will do."

"You know, Captain, there are other ways to live. While you are here in England, perhaps you should take this opportunity to see what we have to offer."

"You are very kind, Lady Winters, but I don't think I could be happy anywhere else. The sea has been my life."

She smiled up at him in a motherly fashion and said, "I was the daughter of a vicar, a very poor vicar. After I grew accustomed to my new life here at Wintersford, I came to like it very well indeed. All I am saying is we do not always recognize when fate has its hand on our shoulders. Keep your eyes open to all the possibilities."

With this, she glided toward the door. After a quick good night to everyone, Lady Winters left the room.

Lady Rotherford covered a yawn and said, "Louisa, it is time for us to go upstairs, too."

"Very well. Captain, it has been a pleasure. Good night, everyone."

When the ladies were gone, Gideon said, "Does Lady Louisa live here, too?"

"Practically," said the earl with a laugh. "She has her own bedroom so that she will not have to go home late at night."

Avery said, "Enough of the ladies. Captain, can I tempt you with a game of billiards?"

"I would not prove much a challenge. I rarely play."

"Grandfather? What about you?"

"Itching for a sound beating, are you? Very well, let us test your mettle. Will you join us, Captain?"

"No, thank you. I think I will follow the ladies' example and go to bed. Good night."

As Gideon climbed the stairs to his room, he stopped again in front of the painting. There was something in the eyes of the girl that drew him. He was not usually given to fancy, but those green eyes enticed him.

He turned at the sound of a door closing and was surprised to see Lady Louisa, candle in hand, floating toward him.

"Lady Rotherford is quite cross, Captain. She cannot stand to lose at cards." Her giggle robbed her words of offense, and he smiled down at her.

"Will I be cast out into the dark night?"

"No, but I would not play with her again—unless you plan to lose. When she was a girl, I caught her cheating on several occasions."

"Really?"

"Oh, nothing too serious. Beware, however, where she seats you the next time. You may have a mirror behind you."

Gideon laughed. "I will be careful, I promise." She was looking up at him with those wonderful green eyes, and he asked, "Lady Louisa, who is the girl in this picture? When I first met you, I thought it might be you."

"Me?"

"Yes, you have eyes very like the girl in the painting—the same lovely color of green."

"I do? You are very kind to say such a thing to an old lady." She squinted at the painting and shook her head. "I am sorry, but I cannot tell exactly which painting it is in this dim light. There are so many here at Wintersford, and Cordelia has a penchant for changing things around all the time. It is probably some distant relation of the Winters clan. Why do you wish to know?"

"No reason. It is just a very pleasant sort of picture, and as I said, the girl in it has eyes the same color as yours, Lady Louisa."

"Merely an artist's viewpoint, I suppose." She covered her mouth as she yawned. "Oh, pardon me. Good night, Captain."

"Good night, ma'am."

Chapter Three

"Grandfather, I have to agree with Grandmother," said Avery across the breakfast table the next morning. He had known convincing his grandfather would be difficult, but he had insisted that they must have the earl's approval of their outrageous scheme to transform the captain into a suitor for Elizabeth.

The earl ran a hand through his gray hair and said, "It is dishonest! You should not try to trick Elizabeth—not that I think you can. I think the captain is a decent man, but Elizabeth will see through his gentlemanly disguise. She will never . . . and what of the captain? Do you seriously think Society will approve of a mere captain—a captain without so much as a ship? They will never accept such a man."

"We all know what Society can be, but think of Elizabeth. You did not hear the things Sir Landon said about her. I think Elizabeth has run out of time. He will do all he can to bring about her fall from grace."

"If what he said was that objectionable, you should have called the man out. That's what I would have done," said his grandfather.

Avery winced at this, since he had been very close to doing just that, but he was saved by his grandmother's next comment.

"It is not just about Sir Landon, Rotherford. I doubt that the hostesses will continue to consider Elizabeth the darling of the *ton* when she has turned down so many suitors over the years. No one likes a girl who is impossible to please."

Avery said quickly, "And how many years has it been?"

"Eight," said Lady Rotherford, her eagle stare spearing her husband, who sat at the opposite end of the table.

"But Elizabeth is still a beauty. No one can deny that!" protested the earl. He took a sip of his morning coffee and shook his head. "Avery, you brought Captain Sparks here with promises of a new ship, not a wife! What the deuce makes you think he wants to wed?"

"Why would he not wish to wed?" demanded his wife. "Elizabeth is a beautiful, wealthy lady. He should count himself fortunate to secure such a wife."

"My point exactly," said her husband. "Any man would consider himself lucky to wed our Elizabeth. There is no need for this sort of desperate matchmaking."

Lady Louisa entered the breakfast room, shutting the door firmly behind her. Putting her finger to her lips, she sailed into the room and took the seat next to the earl.

"I could hear you in the hall." Looking squarely at the earl, she said, "Consider this, Rotherford: our matchmaking efforts are not for the benefit of the captain. They are for the benefit of Elizabeth. She has turned down every man we know. Perhaps it is time to introduce her to someone who does not have a pedigree ten miles long, a man who is not so terribly polished. Perhaps that is the sort of man who will tempt Elizabeth to marry."

"I appreciate your wanting to help Elizabeth, but surely a man such as the captain is not the sort to wed Elizabeth. Would you have her travel around the world with the man? Or worse, would you have her at home, pining away for a husband who is traveling around the world?"

"All I know is this, Rotherford: Elizabeth will not wed where her heart is not engaged. All we can do is present her to the captain. If the captain agrees to our scheme and wins her, we can be confident that she has accepted him because she has fallen in love with him."

"And when she finds out the man she has wed is naught but a common seaman?"

Lady Louisa smiled roguishly and said, "My dear Rotherford, from what I have seen of Captain Sparks, there is nothing common about him."

"Nor will there be by the time we have clothed him and schooled him in the ways of Society. When we have finished with Captain Sparks, he will be the epitome of an English gentleman," said the countess.

"An American English gentleman," said Lady Louisa.

"I can see you are all determined to travel down this road, but I refuse to sit idly by and watch. If you should need me for anything, I will be at the town house in London."

"Rotherford!" said his wife.

The earl set his cup on its saucer and stood up. He walked calmly to the end of the table, kissed his countess on the cheek, and said, "Good-bye, my dear. I do wish you every success, though I have my doubts. Do what you can with the good captain in the weeks before the Season begins. I will see you in London at the end of the month."

When the door had closed, the two women smiled at each other. Avery shook his head and said, "I have never wished to be my grandfather more than at this moment. After listening to his objections, I, too, have my doubts."

The countess said, "Then stiffen your spine, my boy. We have strategies to work out. First, we must convince Captain Sparks. Now that I have met him, I must admit to having my own doubts—not about the success of the plan itself, but about convincing the good captain to agree to the scheme. You know him best, Avery. How should we approach him?"

"And when?" asked Lady Louisa.

"Begging your pardon, my lady. The captain is on his way downstairs right now," said the butler, who was standing guard at the door.

Avery stood up, too, and moved toward the hidden door in the paneling of the breakfast room. "I think I will leave that up to the two of you."

Catching his hand as he passed, his grandmother said, "Avery, you had best stay. Don't you agree, Louisa?" His grandmother's friend nodded, and the countess continued, "He will only laugh at two old ladies."

Lord Winters looked from one woman to the other. With a grimace, he returned to his chair and said petulantly, "Very well, but I want you to know that it is unfair of the two of you to gang up on me like this. Two old ladies, my eye!"

The ladies giggled, but they quickly regained their serious demeanors as the butler opened the door, and the captain entered.

When Gideon saw that the breakfast room was almost full, he felt glad that he had chosen to wear one of the newly altered shirts under his usual coat.

"Good morning," he said.

"Good morning, Captain," they chorused.

Lady Rotherford said, "Please help yourself to the dishes on the sideboard, Captain. Finch, bring a fresh cup of . . ."

"Coffee, please," said Gideon. He finished filling his plate with stewed tomatoes, kidney pie, and a rasher of bacon. Returning to the table, he sat down.

With a glance at the empty chair beside him, he asked, "Lord Winters, can we expect your mother to join us this morning?"

"No, my mother always breakfasts in her room. It is just the four of us."

"Oh? So Lord Rotherford will not be here, either?"

"No, my husband was called away to London on business," said Lady Rotherford.

"I see," said Gideon.

So the earl, the man who was capable of changing the course of his life, was no longer there to discuss the possibility of finding him a new ship. With great effort, he shrugged off his intense disappointment over this disclosure and smiled at the two ladies.

Their responses were perfunctory as they watched him like a couple of . . . *vultures* was the only word that came to mind. A glance in the viscount's direction provided no enlightenment, as he was staring fixedly at the sideboard. Gideon felt a prickling of unease on the back of his neck.

"Actually, the absence of the earl is probably better for our purposes," said Lady Louisa, a nervous giggle escaping her lips.

Now truly on his guard, Gideon asked, "Our purposes?"

The butler entered and placed a steaming cup of coffee beside Gideon's plate.

Lady Rotherford said, "Finch, you may leave us now, and please see that we are not disturbed." When the butler had left the room and shut the door, she continued, "Yes, Captain. We have a proposal to put to you."

"What sort of proposal?" He looked at each of them in turn while a creeping dread settled on his shoulders.

"It is like this, Captain. We know that you have a problem," said Lady Rotherford.

"What with losing your boat," supplied Lady Louisa, adding a hasty, "So sorry for you."

"Yes, yes, but we have a solution to your problem—and should you succeed, then you will also be solving our little problem."

"And Lord Rotherford?" Gideon turned to the viscount and said, "Lord Winters, you indicated that your grandfather could help me. Why is he not here?"

Gideon felt certain he already knew the answer. The earl simply did not wish to help.

"Grandfather was, uh . . ."

"Captain, my husband does not wholly endorse our little proposal. However, I hope you will hear us out."

What else can I do? thought Gideon. "Very well. I am listening."

"Good," said Lady Rotherford. "I am correct in assuming that you have no wife, am I not?"

"That is correct," he replied. He could feel the floor sucking him down like quicksand.

"Good. Lady Louisa and I have a granddaughter who is also unwed." She paused a moment.

When he didn't speak, she gave a little sigh and went on. "Elizabeth has turned down several . . ." This was interrupted by a cough from Lord Winters. After shooting a darkling look at her grandson and clearing her throat, she said, "Several eligible gentlemen. I would not have you thinking that she is on the shelf because she has had no other options."

"I still don't see what this has to do with me."

The countess waved a hand to forestall another comment. "Elizabeth is an heiress in her own right, and upon her marriage, she will control a considerable fortune—that is, her husband will have control of this fortune, to do with as he sees fit."

Gideon rose slowly. With his palms on the table, he leaned forward and glared at the older woman. "Madam, I have done a number of things in my life that I regret, but I am not a fortune hunter!"

"Not a fortune hunter, Captain!" cried Lady Louisa. "Never that!"

"But you are trying to arrange your granddaughter's wedding to a virtual stranger. If I participate in this outrageous scheme, I will become a fortune hunter!"

"You misunderstand, Captain," said Lady Rotherford. "Please sit down and listen to what we have to say."

Gideon thought of storming out of the room. He thought of leaving, but the truth of the matter was that he had no place else to go. Reluctantly, he sat down.

"Thank you. Now let me clarify a few points," said the countess. "First of all, our granddaughter is quite out of our power. Even if we wanted to force a marriage on her, we could not do so. She is free to choose whomever she pleases. So far, she has not found anyone acceptable. We think you might be capable of changing her mind."

Stretching out a plump arm and touching his sleeve, Lady Louisa added, "We only want Elizabeth to be happy."

"What makes you think I can change her mind? I am hardly a ladies' man."

"We are not at all certain that you can, but you are definitely different from the other men who have asked for her hand. And you have the added attraction of having saved her cousin's life."

"You have nothing to lose, old boy," said Lord Winters.

Gideon glared at him before speaking. "Is this what you had in mind all along?"

The viscount shrugged and said, "I must admit that we had discussed the possibility."

"And you led me to believe I was coming here to persuade your grandfather . . . all along, all you wanted was to parade me in front of them, like a damned piece of livestock."

The viscount grinned at him and nodded.

"I ought to knock your lights out," said Gideon.

"Not at my table," said the countess. "Come now, Captain. What we propose is not so outrageous, is it? People marry for money and social position all the time. Surely your United States is not so very different."

"I don't travel in those circles, madam."

"My lady. Really, Captain, you must learn to use our mode of speech, or you will not last an evening in the dangerous waters of London Society."

"London Society?" That prickling sensation was tickling his neck again. The idea of an evening in London

Society filled him with trepidation. Let him face the cannons of an armed ship any day!

"And the beard, Captain. I'm afraid that lovely beard will simply have to go," said Lady Louisa.

"Quite right, Louisa. And the clothes, too. Avery, you will see to that. Take him to London and have him kitted out properly."

"I haven't agreed yet," said Gideon, scrambling for the last shreds of his dignity.

"Really, Captain, do not be a peagoose!" said the countess. "All we ask is that you try. Surely you cannot be so averse to marriage."

"You won't be sorry," said Lady Louisa. "Elizabeth really is a sweet child."

Before he could reply, the countess rose and summoned her friend. "Come along, Louisa. We will leave the gentlemen to make their arrangements to return to London. You'll want to leave tomorrow at the latest, I should think. Only a few short weeks until the Season gets under way, and so very much to accomplish!"

When the two ladies had left them alone, Gideon said, "Damn your eyes, man! How could you let me think . . ."

"Look, it really isn't that unusual, marrying to get what you want, whether it's money, social standing, or a title. People do it all the time here."

"I haven't agreed yet," grumbled Gideon.

"Well, while you are thinking about it, let's go upstairs to my room. While he shaves off that beard, my valet can show you my wardrobe so that you know what will be required for the coming Season."

"If and when I agree, he can shave the beard."

As they went up the stairs, Gideon asked, "Just how ugly is this cousin of yours?"

Avery turned and grinned at him. "Ugly? She's accounted one of the most beautiful women in the *ton*."

"Of course she is."

They paused on the first landing, and Avery strolled

up to the picture of the beautiful girl with the haunting green eyes.

"You have only to see for yourself. It's not like seeing her in person, but the artist tried his best to do her justice."

Gideon's mouth sagged open as he gazed at the girl. She stared back at him, that half smile on her lips, as if she were sharing the joke. In that instant, Gideon knew he would do whatever it took to win that girl.

As insane as it might seem, he had fallen in love with her the first time he laid eyes on her portrait. Suddenly, he couldn't wait to see her in person.

"I only hope your valet's razor is sharp."

Elizabeth flopped across the bed, closing her eyes with a sigh. She had traveled all day from her godmother's house in Leicestershire to the home of Penelope Holloway, her oldest friend.

Like Elizabeth, Penelope had never married, though her reasons were not the same. In the past four years, after her only brother had been wounded in battle on the sea, she had cared for him in their modest home.

Elizabeth often wondered how she would have fared in like circumstances, caring for a crippled brother who spent his days in a Bath chair. Penelope was eternally sunny and optimistic. Elizabeth feared that if she had been cast the same lot, she would be eternally grumpy.

The tiny clock on the mantel began striking. Sitting up, she removed the lacy wrapper she wore over her night rail. It was only ten o'clock, yet the entire household had gone to bed. During the Season in London, her evening would have been beginning at this hour.

Poor Penny, thought Elizabeth. *I must think of some way to steal her away from Whistle's Bend, to let her enjoy the Season, too. Roger would not mind. He could come along, too, for that matter. He might also enjoy getting away from his own dreary problems.*

Elizabeth shook her head. She really must stop feeling sorry for her friends. They didn't feel sorry for themselves. Roger seemed quite content to spend his days tutoring the sons of the local gentry. He was also researching some sort of book on naval history. He was as handsome as ever, but with one leg amputated and the other terribly weakened, Roger went out so seldom it was unlikely that he would ever marry.

Stifling a yawn, Elizabeth turned over and stretched, folding her arms behind her head. She would have to think of some way to convince both of them to go.

Suddenly she smiled. Scrunching down in the bed, she fell asleep, confident that the coming Season would be ever so much more enjoyable than any previous Season.

Elizabeth rose early the next morning. Rain spattered against the small leaded glass in the windows and the wind whistled through the trees. She looked back at the bed with longing, but she stirred the fire and performed her ablutions. Her best chance to catch Roger alone would be in his study while Penelope was busy conferring with the cook and maids. It was not an opportunity to be missed.

Dressed in a serviceable wool gown, Elizabeth made her way down the narrow stairs to the hall below. There was no butler on duty, nor was there a fire in the grate. Her quiet knock on the study door was answered promptly.

Pushing open the door, she watched Roger cover his leg with the plaid lap robe.

"Good morning, Elizabeth."

"Good morning, Roger," she said, entering the room and taking a seat close to his Bath chair. She made certain she sat on his right side. Not only had he lost a leg in battle, the hearing in his left ear had been impaired when his ship blew up.

"How are you this morning?" she asked.

"I'm afraid the damp and cold make my leg ache, but other than that, I am quite well. How did you sleep?"

"Like a baby. Roger, I wanted to talk to you about something."

"You may speak to me on any subject, Elizabeth. I have always considered you my second little sister," he said with a smile.

"You are too kind. I wanted to talk to you about Penny. I think she deserves a treat. I would like her to come to London for the Season. It is selfish of me to want her there, of course, but I hoped you might agree that she needs a chance to get back into Society."

"I couldn't agree more, but I do not know how to manage it. I have told her for four years now that she should go to London for the Season. I insist, I plead, and to no avail. Now, if you have come up with some wizardry to turn the trick, then I will only applaud it."

"I knew you would feel that way," she said, taking his hand and giving it a squeeze. "I believe I have a way, but it will require some sacrifice on your part."

"Only name the sacrifice," he said.

"You must tell her that you wish to go to London to do some research for your book. She will never let you go alone, as we both know. You will both stay with me, of course."

"And how will we get her to leave my side and go about in Society? She will come up with all sorts of reasons why she cannot do so—not a fit wardrobe, no longer fits in—oh, any number of reasons."

"Yes, there is that. Her lack of wardrobe is nothing. She is my size and can avail herself of anything in my wardrobe. The other objections we will deal with when they arise. First, we have to get the two of you to London."

"I still doubt she will agree."

"Then you must be at your most persuasive, Roger. For Penny's sake, and for mine, too! Please say you will do it."

Though he didn't appear sanguine about his success, he smiled at her again. "Very well. I would not wish to spoil your plans."

She leaned forward and kissed his cheek. "You are a dear! And now I will go and tell Penny that you want to see her."

"No, just send the footman to me. I will have him go to her. Otherwise, she will suspect that we are together in this plan."

"Which we are!" laughed Elizabeth as she rose and danced out of the small study.

"Damn it, man! How do you expect me to move in this thing?" demanded Gideon, glaring at the tailor and then at the viscount.

The tailor's nose went up a full inch, and he said, "My lord, if you will explain once more to the captain."

"Gideon, you may as well give in. Everyone wears their coats fitted like that." Avery stood up and turned around. "See, not a single wrinkle across the shoulders."

"I don't give a . . ." Gideon pushed away the tailor's hands and said firmly, "It doesn't wrinkle because it's too blasted tight! You will leave enough room for me to move, do you understand?"

"Very good, sir, but should anyone ask, I beg you not to tell them that you purchased your coat here."

"You have my promise on that!"

The viscount laughed and said, "Good thing the pants are knitted."

"Is it to be that way for all your coats, Captain?" asked the tailor.

"Yes, all of them. I hope boots don't have to be so demmed fitted."

"No, but the hats are." At Gideon's look of horror, the viscount laughed and said, "No, no. Only pulling your leg, Gideon. Oh, that reminds me. Stulz, you said you would have one coat ready today?"

"Yes, it is ready, though it would be better . . . well, never mind that. Yes, I have it."

"Good." Smiling at Gideon, Winters said, "It is time we try you out in Hyde Park on Rotten Row, as they call it."

"Tried me out for what?"

"It is where all the fashionables go to see and be seen. We will collect our horses at the stable and go there this afternoon. London is thin of company, of course, but there will still be some people out and about. You fit in quite well with the gentlemen at my club. Now it is time we tried you out on the ladies."

Thinking of those eyes, Gideon asked, "Will . . . that is, are you expecting anyone in particular to be there?"

"No, no. She is still visiting friends."

"Oh, then that's good," said Gideon.

He would not be meeting Elizabeth that afternoon. The knowledge left him feeling both disappointed and relieved at the same time. This being his first venture into polite feminine circles, he did not yet feel equal to meeting Elizabeth. Still, he was a man of action, and anticipation was wearing thin.

When Lord Winters had offered him the choice of the stables at Wintersford, Gideon had selected a big gelding. The horse was not terribly handsome, and his gait was a little jarring, but he was large enough to easily carry the long-legged captain. More importantly, the groom had said that the horse had an aversion to jumping. This suited Gideon, who had never done a great deal of riding.

"Are you all right on that beast?" asked the viscount as they entered the street on the way to the park.

"Don't worry. Roman and I will be fine," he said, patting the glossy neck to soothe both himself and the horse.

"You know, it doesn't hurt to have a more showy animal when one is trying to impress the ladies. You know the sort of thing. A half-tamed stallion dancing this way and that."

"Yes, and leaving me sitting on the ground after one too many this way or thats," said Gideon.

They entered the park, and Gideon asked, "Is there anyone in particular you wish me to meet?"

"Not anyone in particular, but I expect we will encounter some of the hostesses, and you will feel better about the coming Season if you have already met some of them. Oh, here comes Lady Beresford right now. That's her daughter—her married daughter—with her."

The viscount angled his horse toward the oncoming carriage as it rolled to a stop.

"Good afternoon, Lady Beresford, Mrs. Ford. How delightful to see you," he said, bowing slightly.

"Lord Winters," said both ladies. The elder then asked, "Are you already here for the Season?"

"Just here on a short visit. Allow me to introduce my friend, Gideon Sparks, Captain Gideon Sparks. Lady Beresford and Mrs. Ford."

Gideon bowed slightly, and the ladies nodded.

The older woman's mouth sagged open and she placed her hand over her heart as she said, "Sir, are you not the man who saved the viscount's life?"

Gideon opened his mouth, but Avery jumped in with, "Indeed he is! You would not be speaking to me right now were it not for Captain Sparks."

"Then we are very indebted to you, Captain," said the younger lady. She giggled and said coyly, "Especially my sister, Lady Anne. She will be delighted to meet you and thank you for saving our Lord Winters."

"Belinda," hissed her mother.

Hiding his confusion, Gideon said, "I look forward to meeting her, too."

"Well, we mustn't keep you. I shall be sending you an invitation to a little party, Winters. Be sure to bring Captain Sparks along."

"Thank you, my lady. Good afternoon."

When the carriage was out of earshot, Gideon said, "What was that all about?"

"I'm afraid I raised some hopes last year with the younger sister. Well, perhaps not Lady Anne's hopes, but definitely her mother's hopes, and when all is said and done, that means the same thing."

"It sounds to me like this Season thing is rather like going for a ride in a swamp," said Gideon. "Only here, there are no snakes."

Avery laughed and said, "Oh, there are snakes, old boy. There are definitely snakes."

Chapter Four

Gideon shifted in the saddle and glanced up at the morning sun. He brushed a leaf from the sleeve of his new coat. The action reminded him of his clean-shaven face, and he touched his chin. It had become a habit in the past three weeks as he was transformed, at least on the outside, into a fashionable gentleman.

He found his new persona almost impossible to grasp, but he had to admit that it had opened doors for him in London. Since their plan called for him to fit in with Society, Winters had taken him to his club and introduced him to many men of wealth and power. Gideon was comforted with the possibility that if he should fail to win the affections of the beautiful Elizabeth, these new connections might very well lead him to a fresh start.

After being measured and fitted for an entire wardrobe, he and the viscount had returned to Wintersford for the completion of Gideon's renovation, as the blunt countess called it. He was learning to fence, drive a pair of bloods, and dance.

Gideon felt that his progress on this last social grace was not going very well. He felt ridiculous practicing a waltz with Lady Louisa for his partner. Lady Winters, who would have been more suitable, played the pianoforte as they lumbered around the room while the countess barked orders.

To give her credit, Lady Louisa was an enthusiastic partner, but her age led her to require frequent breaks from the strenuous exercise. Lord Winters would sit on the side of the room and make clever comments, causing Lady Louisa to giggle like a schoolgirl, draining away what extra breath she possessed. Lady Rotherford had finally banished her grandson from the room.

When not being instructed in how to dance or balance a plate on one knee while drinking tea, Gideon preferred to escape outside. This morning, Gideon was on horseback, enjoying the crisp air. It was almost noon, and his stomach was protesting the lack of food. He turned in the direction of Wintersford, or so he thought, but now he was unsure.

Gideon pulled back on the reins and ducked down to look beyond the thick trees that lined the path he was following. Across a small pasture was a large house.

Gideon patted the gelding's neck and turned him, saying, "Someone over there should be able to tell us how to get back to Wintersford and food."

A few minutes later, Gideon slid to the ground and led his horse toward the front door. Unlike his arrival at Wintersford, his presence was not met with footmen and a butler, so he looped the reins over the gatepost. Just as he was about to knock, he heard the faint sound of someone singing. After tying his horse to the fence, he went around the side of the house. The voice, clearly feminine, grew louder as he walked.

I saw a young maiden in the valley far below
How can you lie to me,
I, who would die for ye,
How can you do a poor maiden so?

When he rounded the corner, he stopped, astounded to discover a large, formal garden, much grander than the house merited. So taken was he by the beauty of the garden that he forgot about the singing. He strolled down a path, his boots crunching on the gravel.

It was too early for flowers, except a few crocuses, but the greenery was lush and varied. He touched a large leaf that had a very tropical appearance.

"'Scuse me, guvner. Can I help you?" With a grunt, a short, round man straightened and faced him. He held a spade in one dirty hand and a bucket in the other.

"What? Oh, yes, thank you. I am staying at Wintersford, and I'm afraid I have gotten turned around. Can you tell me how to get back from here?"

"Wintersford? Oh, you've gotten all turned about, you 'ave. You need t' go back to the front o' the 'ouse and down the drive. At th' end, turn to yer right. When you get to the crossroads, turn to yer left. Ye can't miss it."

This could not have been the source of the very feminine singing he had just heard, thought Gideon. He looked beyond the gardener to see Lady Louisa clambering to her feet. He hurried forward to assist her.

"Lady Louisa, what a pleasant surprise. This must be the dower house you spoke about."

"Good afternoon, Captain. Yes, this is the dower house of my late husband's estate. The main house is beyond that copse of trees." Pushing her gray hair out of her eyes, she said, "I am sorry that you find me in such disarray. I arrived home this morning to find that one of my contacts in the West Indies had sent me a shipment of seeds. Hibiscus, to be exact. I am clearing a spot for them."

"A pretty flower, if I remember correctly," he said.

"Oh! You have seen them in person?"

"I think so."

"How wonderful! My friend is quite a good artist and drew a picture of the flower." She took off her glove and pulled a piece of paper out of her apron pocket. "Is this the one you recall?"

"Yes, that's the one. I just remember being quite taken by their size and color," he replied.

"Yes, she says they come in several colors, so it will be

a surprise to see what comes up where. But where are my manners? You must come inside for some tea."

She took his arm to lead him toward the house, but when she glanced back at the overturned earth with longing, Gideon disengaged himself and said, "I would like that, but I cannot stay. I was really just trying to find my way back to Wintersford. Your gardener gave me directions."

"Would you like me to send a footman with you?"

"No, thank you. I can manage now."

"If you are sure, then I shall return to my digging."

"Certainly. Will I see you again before I leave for London later in the week?"

"Tonight. Didn't Cordelia tell you? She has planned a dinner tonight to introduce you to local Society."

He shook his head, and she said, "You must forgive her. She rarely thinks about consulting others when making her plans. Yes, it promises to be a pleasant debut for you—very informal and comfortable. I would not miss it for the world." Shading her eyes from the sun, she smiled up at him, her green eyes shining with mischief.

"Should I be wary of this dinner?" he asked.

"No, no, only I think there is to be some dancing. Quite impromptu, but you will finally have a partner or two worthy of your energy."

Gideon stood at attention, took her hand, and gave an elegant bow. On rising, he said, "I cannot imagine another partner more worthy than you, my dear Lady Louisa."

"Oh," came the breathless reply. Then she giggled and said, "Captain, you are a rogue!"

"Is that a good thing? I mean, where your granddaughter is concerned?"

She was thoughtful for a moment. Then that smile broke forth, and she patted his sleeve. "I think it might be a very good thing indeed. Only time will tell. We must learn patience."

"I have never been a very patient man, my lady."

"Sometimes we have no choice in the matter," she said. "Good afternoon, Captain."

"Good afternoon, Lady Louisa. Until tonight."

"There is nothing for it, my lady. This wheel will never make it all the way. If we detour ten miles, we can spend the night at home and have it fixed properly before going on to Mrs. Lightfoot's house tomorrow."

The coachman delivered the verdict with a grimace. Elizabeth sighed, but she agreed to the proposed detour.

"Only let us not go to Wintersford, Mr. Cochran. It is only for one night, and I would much prefer not having to deal with the entire family. We will go to the dower house instead. Lady Louisa will not be put out with the suddenness of our arrival."

"But at her ladyship's small stable, I won't have the means t' fix the wheel, my lady," said the coachman.

"True. Very well, but I am spending the night at the dower house, so you must keep it quiet when you take the carriage over to Wintersford to have it fixed."

"I'll do better than that, my lady," said the man with a grin. "I'll take th' wheel off at the dower house and take only that back to Wintersford with me. Less people will notice my return that way."

"Thank you, Mr. Cochran."

Elizabeth climbed back inside the large traveling carriage, and they resumed their journey, going slowly to prevent the cracked wheel from breaking completely.

Gideon rode back to Wintersford with a light heart. Lady Louisa had to be one of the kindest ladies he had ever met. She made him feel glad about the whole mad scheme, made him feel hopeful.

He went straight to the dining room and was relieved to

find it empty except for an array of dishes waiting on the sideboard. He helped his plate and poured a glass of cool ale from a pitcher before sitting down and diving in.

He had little time to himself these days, and he should have enjoyed himself, being alone, but he was too on edge to appreciate the treat. Since agreeing to this conspiracy, he found that spare time had become his enemy. It was all part and parcel of that innate impatience that ran through his veins. He hated surprises. He preferred being the one to lead, to make things happen.

For almost three weeks, he had been pushed, prodded, and molded into someone he didn't know. While he applauded the goal, he was ready to begin, ready to put all these plans to the test—ready, he admitted privately, to meet Lady Elizabeth Winters.

Gideon pushed away from the table. It wouldn't be long now. Until then, as Lady Louisa had said, he would have to learn patience.

He left the dining room and mounted the stairs of the large manor house, pausing at the painting as he always did. Gideon looked around to be certain that he was alone. Finch had caught him gazing raptly at Lady Elizabeth one day and had looked at him very strangely.

At the moment, no one was about, and he stepped as close as he could to the image of the beautiful girl on the chestnut horse. Dark, lustrous curls hung loose to her waist. Her large eyes glowed with amusement. He could almost hear her laughter.

"Soon," he murmured.

A door opened and closed and a maid came down the hall. When she passed, he was strolling casually to his room.

Lady Louisa dropped the spade and exclaimed, "Elizabeth! What on earth are you doing here?"

"I am not really here," she said.

"What is that supposed to mean?" asked Louisa as she gave her granddaughter a distracted kiss on the cheek.

"I was on the way to Mother's when the carriage wheel cracked. Mr. Cochran said it would be best to stop at Wintersford to have it repaired."

"But you are here, not there," came her grandmother's confused reply.

"Yes, because I did not wish to get the entire house into a state by my sudden appearance. You will remember that when I left, Grandmother was less than pleased with me."

Lady Louisa smiled and nodded knowingly. "And you did not wish to hear her lectures, so you came here."

Elizabeth grinned and said, "Where I know I will be coddled and welcomed by my sweet Mimi."

"Minx! Now you are trying to get around me. Come along. Let us go inside for tea." Lady Louisa looked up at the sky and said, "What time is it?"

"Three o'clock."

"Oh dear, I have been out here in the sun all day! My freckles will be popping out all over."

"Your freckles are delightful," said Elizabeth, opening the door for her grandmother.

"Cordelia says freckles are the sign of a farmer's wife."

"A tenant farmer's wife, to be precise," laughed Elizabeth. "You see, I have that lecture memorized. Why should I go to Wintersford to hear it again?"

"Go to . . . oh dear. I should be getting ready."

"Ready?"

"Yes, Cordelia is having a little gathering of the neighbors, and I am invited, of course."

"Then you most certainly should go, Mimi. I will be fine here by myself. I need the rest."

"No, I shan't go. I would much prefer to remain here with you, my dear."

"If you wish, but I will not be very good company. I mean to go to bed early. I'm going up to wash my face and change my gown. Then I will come down and join you for tea."

"That's fine. I will just send Cordelia a note."

Lady Louisa sat down at the small desk in the corner of the snug drawing room.

Dear Cordelia,

Elizabeth has arrived on my doorstep for the night! I feel I should stay here to make certain she doesn't change her mind and ride over to Wintersford. The time is not quite ripe for her to meet our captain. Please remember every last detail to tell me tomorrow.

Louisa

She sealed the envelope and took it to the footman for immediate delivery. As she watched him depart, she shook her head. She had been looking forward to watching the captain dance with the young ladies. To her, he was always charming. She only hoped others would view him in the same light.

Finally, it was time to dress for dinner. Gideon went up to his room and shrugged out of the riding coat that he still considered too snug. He hung the dark blue garment on the back of the Sheraton chair at the small desk. Then he sauntered toward the fire, holding his hands out to the warmth. Late March, and it was still cold. This was nothing like Charleston, where he had grown up. Still, he found he was looking forward to being in London in the spring. Spring, the time of new life.

Gideon chuckled at his own absurdity. He was mooning around over a girl who very probably would take one look at him, or hear one word from him, and laugh herself silly. What the devil was he thinking, he asked himself, to believe that a spoiled beauty of English Society would consider wedding the likes of him?

He turned to look at his image in the cheval glass and studied his face dispassionately. Not too hideous without the beard. The skin beneath it was finally starting to look like the rest of his face. His square jaw had the tendency to jut out when he was annoyed, but his nose was straight and so were his teeth. His eyes were good, he supposed, but then, how could a fellow know what a woman might think of all this? To him, women had always been more mysterious than the sea.

Mallard, his new valet, supervised the filling of the copper bathtub. When the footmen had departed, the valet turned to Gideon and said, "Will there be anything else, Captain?"

"No, that's all. I can manage."

Gideon stripped off his dressing gown and smalls before easing into the steaming water. Being quite tall, his knees were almost under his chin. Still, a bath such as this was quite a luxury. He soaped his body and scrubbed his hair. Picking up a copper ladle, he poured water over his head.

He and Lord Winters were to leave for London in a few days. The elusive Elizabeth was supposed to be there by the end of the week. Finally, he would meet her, speak to her. It was odd being in love with a mere picture.

He had soaked up every word her grandmothers and cousin had said about her. Lady Rotherford had cautioned him time and again that he must be the perfect gentleman if he wished to win Elizabeth. She had stressed that any familiarity on his part would be damning to his cause. Lady Louisa, on the other hand, was more inclined to humor. She warned him that while Elizabeth's suitors had all behaved as gentlemen to her, they had not won her heart. The implication was clear—he had to be bold enough, but not too bold.

Gideon muttered a curse. Never had he gone to such trouble over a woman. But as Lord Winters was prone to remind him, it was not just Elizabeth he wanted to secure. It was also a new life and fortune.

As Gideon cleaned his nails, he thought about it. It rankled that he was planning to wed for money. Perhaps that was the way the wealthy did things—not just in England, but back home, too. He knew this, and yet he would not have Elizabeth think that her wealth was the reason he was wedding her.

With another muttered curse, he rose and stepped out of the tub. He dried himself with a large towel and then wrapped it around his waist.

Perhaps when he met the wench, he would not like her in the least. Then his problems would be simplified and multiplied at the same time. Simplified because he would not marry a woman he did not care for, and multiplied because he would once again be a man far from home without a cent to his name.

Gideon's valet entered and placed his shaving implements on the dressing table. He waited patiently while Gideon sat down. When he had been shaved, Gideon dressed. When it came to the cravat, he allowed the valet to tie it.

Gideon glanced at his image and said, "Thank you, Mallard. I could never learn to tie my cravat like that."

The dignified valet colored with pleasure and said, "I am happy to know that my service is satisfactory, Captain Sparks." He helped Gideon put on his coat, smoothing the cloth across the broad shoulders with care. "There, sir. I believe you are ready now."

With a nod, Gideon left the room and made his way downstairs to the drawing room, where the countess was waiting for him.

His "lessons" with the countess took the form of cards for an hour before dinner. Lady Rotherford would talk nonstop about London and the latest gossip. Secretly, Gideon thought that this was merely a ruse to distract him so that he would lose track of the cards. Sometimes

Gideon slipped, but most of the time, he won. This would, in turn, distract and irritate the countess, and she would demand to know how he knew which cards she held.

Gideon found that his mere smile could serve to irritate her even further. He was not about to tell her that the way he came to own his first ship had been through winning a card game.

This evening was no different, despite the fact that guests would be arriving soon. Dressed in another of her black silk gowns, Lady Rotherford was already seated at the small table in front of the windows.

"Good evening, Captain," she said in answer to his bow.

"Good evening, my lady," came the proper reply.

Lady Rotherford began to deal the twelve cards for their game of piquet. "I received a letter from my old friend Lady Bostwick this morning. Her husband is in politics," she added, her nose rising minutely.

"Really? Tory or Whig?" he asked, picking up the last of his twelve cards. Seeing that there were no face cards, he added, "Carte blanche, my lady."

"Carte . . . very well, that is ten points to you," she said through clenched teeth.

"Thank you. Tory or Whig?" he said again, gazing at her hawklike nose and tight lips.

"How the deuce should I know? Or care," she added. "Sequence," she declared, somewhat mollified.

"I thought it might make a difference in your story. But if not, then do go on."

"Lady Bostwick has two sons, both quite handsome and quite empty-headed. One of them, at least, has had the good sense to wed a young lady who is quite bright and will keep him from harm."

"And the other?" he said, drawing a card.

"The other has gone and wed an opera dancer, of all things! Point!" she said gleefully.

"Perhaps the young man fell in love with her."

"In love? What has that to say in the matter? At least he is not Bostwick's heir. That would have been most unsuitable. As it is, Lady Bostwick is bemoaning the fact that her son and this person are being shipped off to the West Indies, where he can pretend to manage some interests they have there."

"She will miss him," said Gideon.

"She will miss being able to tell the boy what to do, is more like. Lady Bostwick, bless her soul, is the most manipulative lady I have ever met. Her two sons have kept her happy for years because she has been able to tell them what to do, what to wear, and so on. Now, she is left with no one. How wretched she must feel!" she added gleefully. Then, "Still, I daresay she will find some other relative to bully."

Gideon smiled and took the final trick, causing the countess to grind her teeth.

"A dear friend of yours, I see."

"No, but a long-time acquaintance," she replied. Her concentration was on gathering the cards, and she missed the gleam of mischief in his eyes.

Rising, Gideon asked, "May I pour you another glass of wine, my lady?"

"Yes. Tell me, how did you know . . ."

"I don't know. I simply guess and often I am lucky," he said, glancing over his shoulder as he poured two glasses of wine.

The countess was arranging the cards in the deck. He grinned. Lady Louisa had warned him about the countess.

Returning to the table, he said, "If you will pardon my saying so, Lady Rotherford, you depend too much on skill and remembering the cards. You should trust your instincts like I do."

She offered the deck before dealing. He cut it in two and pretended not to notice when the countess casually replaced the two halves in the same order. She was a wicked old woman.

Accompanying his mother, Lord Winters entered the room and said, "Enjoying your game? Grandmother is not fleecing you, is she?"

"We only play for points—and the honor of winning," said Gideon.

"And he is winning again anyway, but I think my luck is turning. Point," she announced. "And sequence."

"Your luck really has changed," said Gideon.

"Squire Fanshaw, Mrs. Fanshaw, and Miss Fanshaw," announced Finch.

"Saved by the butler," murmured Gideon.

Gideon rose and in moments was swept into a dizzying array of introductions—new names and new faces.

Over the next half an hour, he met a number of very pretty girls. Somehow, their older relatives managed to melt away after the introductions, leaving Gideon and the viscount to entertain the girls.

Miss Price possessed herself of his arm and pressed her breast against him. With a deep sigh, she said, "Captain, I think you must be the bravest man I have ever met."

"The bravest man who has ever come to Wintersford," said her younger sister, Miss April.

A Miss Haversham gushed, "And you, Lord Winters, coming so close to perishing! The very thought just makes me shiver!" She shivered while gazing into the viscount's eyes.

He laughed and said, "But you do it so well!"

The girls tittered at this witticism. Suddenly, Gideon just wanted to get away from all of them. He was relieved when Finch announced dinner.

The dinner was more sumptuous than usual. The soup and its removes of salmon and lobster were followed by leg of lamb and venison. By the third course, Gideon was already stuffed, but he continued to eat. He also drank a great deal. It seemed everyone wanted to take wine with the man who had saved the viscount. By the time the dessert was produced, Gideon was not certain he would be able to walk.

Miss Fanshaw sat opposite him. Her demeanor was quite different from the lively young ladies he had met before dinner. Seated between the squire and some boy with red hair and spots, she spoke so softly, Gideon could not even hear her voice.

Miss Fanshaw was not terribly pretty, but he found he was more interested in her than in the talkative Miss Price, who sat beside him and never closed her mouth, even while chewing. He found himself hoping that Lady Elizabeth's behavior would more closely resemble Miss Fanshaw's than Miss Price's behavior.

When the gentlemen were left to their port, Gideon heaved a sigh of relief. There was talk floating around him, but he did not have to pay close attention. The squire, upon hearing that Gideon hailed from South Carolina, asked if he owned a plantation. When Gideon said no, that he didn't have any land, the squire wandered away.

"Come in, Mr. Cochran. You wished to speak to me?" asked Elizabeth.

The coachman, hat in hand, stepped lightly into the hall. "I am sorry to disturb you, my lady, but I thought you would want to know that Buttermilk has had her foal—a fine little lad, th' same color as his mum."

"Really? Oh, now I wish I had gone to Wintersford with you! When did it happen?"

"Two days ago."

"Oh, I have to go and see him," said Elizabeth, looking over her shoulder toward the drawing room. It was dark already—not the time for a proper lady to go wandering about, even in the country.

"I would be happy t' take you over."

"No, no. You have had a very long day, and I haven't even asked if you managed to fix the wheel."

"Yes, m'lady. We will be ready at nine o'clock in th' morning, just as you requested. But I don't mind taking you back over to Wintersford."

"No, it can wait. Thank you for coming to tell me, Mr. Cochran. Good night."

The coachman bowed slightly and backed away. Elizabeth rejoined her grandmother in the drawing room and tried to settle on her novel again. After a few minutes, she yawned and stretched.

"Tired already, my dear?" asked Lady Louisa.

"It has been a very long day. I think I will just go up to bed to read."

"An early night will do you good."

Elizabeth kissed her grandmother's cheek and hurried away. She went to the wardrobe in her room and dragged an old box out. She rummaged through it until she found the items she was searching for—a pair of trousers and one of Avery's old shirts. She took off her dress and put on the old clothes. She pulled on some half boots and then jammed a battered hat on top of her head, covering her curls and the last vestiges of Lady Elizabeth.

She blew her image a kiss and then stole out of the house.

Finally, it was time to rejoin the ladies. Upon entering the drawing room, Gideon was swept away by the young ladies who were overseeing the rolling back of the rugs so that they could dance.

Lady Winters, knowing his limited abilities, struck up a simple quadrille. There were enough people for two squares, and Gideon had no difficulty following the movements of the other dancers.

"A waltz!" called Miss Price when the first set was over. She then headed toward Gideon.

He turned and found himself face to face with Miss Fanshaw.

While he was apologizing, she said, "Would you like to dance with me, Captain?"

Returning her friendly smile, he said, "I . . . why, yes, I would, Miss Fanshaw."

He took her in his arms and the music began. His first waltz, proper waltz, with a proper young lady. He remembered not to hold her too tight.

"I will not break," she said softly.

He looked down to find her grinning at him. "I am sorry," he said. "I am not much used to dancing."

"Just relax, Captain. If you are too stiff, we shan't be able to dance properly."

The music started, and Gideon concentrated for several minutes, silently counting out the steps of the dance.

"You do this very well, Captain. You have a natural grace."

"And you are very kind, Miss Fanshaw." They made another turn, and he began to relax. "You are not like the others."

"Others?"

"Miss Price and her sister."

She actually giggled at this. "That is because I am not on the hunt for a husband."

"No? I thought all young ladies were looking for husbands."

She shook her head and said, "Can you keep a secret?" He nodded and she continued, "I am already betrothed, although it has not been announced. I am to wed the local curate, once I have had my Season in London and he has spoken to his uncle about becoming the vicar in the village where his uncle's estate is located."

"Congratulations to you both. Your curate is a singularly lucky fellow."

"A very pretty compliment, sir. I thank you," she said.

"I have never met anyone from America before. I did not know they could be so charming."

"Thank you for saying so. I fear I am a bit too unpolished for gatherings such as these. And London, to be quite frank, scares me to death." *London and Lady Elizabeth,* he thought privately.

"You will do very well, Captain. Society is always willing to forgive a little faux pas when the culprit is handsome and charming."

The music ended, and Miss Price claimed him. He danced with every young lady present, one after the other. The air in the drawing room was becoming oppressive. Servants entered and opened the doors to the wide stone terrace.

Gideon noticed Miss Fanshaw slipping outside, and he followed. She was the only sensible female he had encountered all evening.

He found her on the far end, gazing at the bright moon. When he stepped closer, he saw a tear run down her cheek.

She jumped when he spoke. "Is something wrong?"

She shook her head, but another tear trickled down her cheek.

"I am just being silly," she whispered as she accepted his handkerchief to wipe her eyes. Clearing her throat, she said more firmly, "I told Harold that I would look at the moon every night that we were apart and think of him doing the same. Silly, I know. But that is the type of thing a girl in love says."

"I don't think it silly at all. I find it heartening somehow to know that such devotion exists."

"Now I suspect you are fibbing, Captain, but it is very polite of you to do so. So you are going to be in London for the Season?" He nodded and she said, "Then I will probably see you there. Since I have revealed my little secret, we will be able to dance the occasional waltz without any awkwardness between us."

"Awkwardness?"

"Yes, you know. Neither of us will have to dazzle the other with a show of coyness or gallantry. We can simply be comfortable with each other."

Gideon smiled and said, "Then I shall certainly seek you out, Miss Fanshaw."

"Captain Sparks, Lady Rotherford wishes to speak to you," called Lady Winters.

He turned in surprise. "To me?"

"Yes, she, uh, said it had, uh, I don't know precisely, but . . ."

Gideon turned to Miss Fanshaw and excused himself. When he entered the drawing room, Lady Rotherford was waiting for him.

"Did nothing I said to you sink in, Captain?" she hissed.

Frowning, he said, "I beg your pardon, my lady."

"What would you do if Miss Fanshaw entered the room and declared that you had compromised her?"

"Compromised her? At a country gathering, in a matter of five minutes on the terrace?" he said, his voice as cold as hers. "I would think everyone would say I made a very quick job of seducing her."

"Shh, Captain!" said Lady Winters, who was trying to shield them from the other guests.

"Lady Winters, I am sorry if my plain speaking disturbs you, but I will not be treated like a child." Glaring at the countess, he said, "Not by anyone."

"You are supposed to follow our instructions," she said, glaring back at him, not giving an inch.

"The lessons are over, countess. I'll do as I damned well please, and you and all the rest of your family can go hang!"

"Captain!" whispered Lady Winters as he turned and stepped outside again.

Miss Fanshaw was gone. Gideon supposed she had entered by another of the open doors. It was for the best.

He had no real interest in pursuing her, and she certainly had none in him. He strode down the steps and out to the stables. Looking at his feet, Gideon hesitated. Dancing shoes were hardly suitable for riding. Taking the tack by his horse's stall, he threw the saddle on the horse's back.

"Blast! I told that groom to replace the girth."

Soothing his temper with a string of oaths, Gideon looked down the row of stalls. Light was coming from one of them, and he hurried toward it.

"You're a pretty one," he heard the groom murmur. Gideon shook his head. He could hardly call the slight figure in the stall with the mare a groom. He was only chest high.

"You, lad!"

The boy jumped and the mare snorted, moving between him and her foal. The groom soothed her and then turned. Giving the rim of his hat a tug, he stepped closer.

"Go and fetch me a new girth, or a new saddle."

The boy lifted his head slightly and then ducked his face again, mumbling something.

Impatience led Gideon to say, "Go on, boy! I'm going for a ride."

"At night, sir?" said the boy in a low, gruff voice.

"That is really none of your business. Just get me another saddle for Roman."

Again there was that tug at his hat, but Gideon had the strangest sensation that it was not a gesture of servitude.

"What's your name?" he demanded when the lad came back, dragging the saddle.

"El . . . bert."

He uttered an oath and said, "Here, give me that. You'll never manage to throw it on his back. How the devil do you work in the stables when you are so small?"

Elizabeth stepped back and watched him throw the saddle onto the horse's back. His shoulders were so broad, but there was no padding there. It was all muscle.

She didn't know who he was, but she was very willing to enjoy studying him.

"So what do you do here, Elbert?" he asked as he reached under the horse and took the cinch.

"Dunno, sir. Mostly I sweep up." She plucked up her courage and asked, "Where are you from, sir? You don't sound like anyone I know."

"I'm from America."

Gideon fastened the cinch and led the horse out of the stall. After swinging up on the horse's back, he glanced at Elizabeth and flipped her a coin that she managed to catch.

"Thank you, sir," said the boy.

Gideon kicked the gelding's sides, and the big head swung around in surprise.

"Come on," he said. "A little ride in the moonlight will not kill you."

Then with a turn of the reins and another kick, the horse trotted away from the lights and into the night.

Chapter Five

Elizabeth awoke, startled by her vivid dreams. A smile played on her lips as she recalled the tall, handsome stranger who had flipped her the coin. In her disguise, she hadn't dared to stare at him openly, but what she had seen had been very pleasing. Tall, so very tall. He had swung up on Roman's back with ease.

In her dream, he had reached down for her and carried her away. She snuggled down in the bed at the memory. Not memory, she reminded herself. In truth, he had not even touched her. But in her dream, the embrace on horseback had been followed by a kiss that left her breathless.

She licked her lips. She had never been kissed like that, but somehow, it had seemed so natural—so real. The man was a stranger to her. She would surely have remembered meeting a man as tall and handsome as he was.

She smiled. In another week, she would be in London. The Season would be under way, and she would have a mission this year. She would search high and low for the elegant gentleman with the colorful language.

From America, he had said. *Please,* she thought, *do not let him go home before I make his acquaintance wearing a proper gown!*

Elizbeth arrived at her mother's house shortly before dark. She was greeted with the news that both her mother and stepfather had gone out to a prayer meeting for one of their flock who was dying.

The sunshine of the morning had given way to drizzle and cold. Elizabeth asked for a tray in her room. After ordering that the meager fire be stoked, she allowed her maid to dress her for bed. The supper was merely a cold collation, but it tasted good after the damp carriage ride.

As night settled in, the heat from the fire was not sufficient to ward off the chill. Elizabeth finally put down the book she had brought to read—a romantic tale that her stepfather would condemn utterly—and she climbed into bed, pulling the covers up to her chin.

She didn't know if it was really colder in this house or if it was merely the repressive atmosphere. Her stepfather was a devout follower of the Methodist sect. He disapproved of all worldly things, and this included his stepdaughter. They had never seen eye to eye. She had been only four when her mother wed Steven Lightfoot, but with childish fervor, she had taken to him in dislike. He had certainly never been a father to her, and to this day, she persisted in calling him Mr. Lightfoot.

Though she now admitted that her mother seemed content, she still found the man exacerbating. Elizabeth planned to stay several days with her mother, but she was uncertain that she could bear to be in Mr. Lightfoot's company for so long.

Hearing the sound of an arrival downstairs, Elizabeth blew out the candle and pretended to be asleep. It would be better to wait until morning before speaking to her mother. She, and hopefully her patience, should be fresher.

Mrs. Lightfoot was still a beauty. Her hair was turning gray, but her skin was clear and smooth, and her eyes were the same sparkling green as those of her mother, Lady Louisa, and her daughter, Elizabeth. She wore only black with not a trace of lace or decoration. The neckline of her dresses gave no hint of the generous décolletage that had inspired many a poem during her own debut into Society.

As she often told Elizabeth, she had chosen her first husband wisely, as befitted an obedient daughter. Elizabeth had asked her once why she had wed the heir to the Earl of Rotherford, and her mother had responded that she had simply obeyed her parents. Knowing this, Elizabeth was always surprised that she had accepted Steven Lightfoot. Perhaps it really had been a love match.

Elizabeth rose early, hoping to catch her mother before she began her day of good works. She knew that her stepfather always rode out immediately after breakfast and would not return until afternoon. She found her mother in the breakfast room.

"Elizabeth, my dear daughter, how wonderful to have you home again."

In deference to her plans, Elizabeth did not remind her mother that she did not consider this her home.

Kissing her mother's cheek, she said, "It is so good to see you, Mother. You are looking very well."

"Aren't you kind to say so? We were out so late last night, I was quite done in. But there, I should not complain when we are doing the Lord's bidding."

"I suppose not. How is the man you went to see?"

"Not good. I fear he will not last the week, but only the Lord knows the answer to such questions."

"True. Have you been keeping busy?" asked Elizabeth, trying to turn the subject.

"Yes, yes. Idle hands, you know. I have taken up a new needlework. That is, it is new to me. I will have to show you. It is done with gold thread. Most challenging, I assure you."

Elizabeth smiled. If her mother could be accused of having one passion, it would be needlework. Never one to sit idly, she always had a needle in her hand.

Elizabeth could not refrain from teasing, however, and

she pretended to be shocked. "Golden thread! How extravagant!"

"No, no, nothing like that. I am working on new altar cloths for the chapel. But I must admit that I am enjoying myself immensely," she confessed.

"And why should you not enjoy yourself?" Elizabeth demanded. Immediately, her mother's excitement died, and she wished she could swallow her comment.

Inspiration struck, and she said quickly, "I mean, are you not supposed to enjoy serving the Lord?"

Her mother's guilty brow cleared and she said, "Yes, you are right, dear. I should enjoy doing His bidding. Now, enough about me. How is my mother?"

"Mimi is doing very well. She is still digging in that garden of hers. When you visit her in June, you will be much amazed at how large it is. She has had the gardener working all winter, adding flower beds for all her new species. You should ask her for some seeds to add to your own collection."

"Oh, I prefer to leave all that to our own gardener. I never shared my mother's enthusiasm for plants, you know."

"Yes, I know," said Elizabeth.

A silence followed. Her mother picked up her pencil and continued making notes on the paper beside her plate. Elizabeth put a piece of toast on her plate. Tearing it in pieces, she nibbled a bit while trying to decide if the time was right to approach her mother about coming to London.

"I have been visiting with Penelope and Roger this past week, you know."

Her mother set aside her spectacles and looked up. "Yes, dear. You said so in your letter."

"Oh, so I did."

Her mother smiled and then continued her task.

"They have agreed to come to London for a month. I am so looking forward to it."

"That is nice, dear."

"Penelope has not been since . . . since Roger was wounded."

"She has been busy with more important things. She has had responsibilities."

Elizabeth wondered if she was only imagining the reproach in her mother's comment. She knew her mother considered her a frivolous person. She was not, of course. She donated a great deal of money to all sorts of charities.

Her mother rose and said, "I really must be going, Elizabeth. I have the parish poor to visit. Would you like to come along?"

"If you need my help, Mother."

"I am not the one who needs help, dear. We have a duty to help others who are less fortunate."

"Yes, Mother, and I do what I can when I am at home, at Wintersford. Since I am not familiar with your neighbors, I wondered if they would be made uncomfortable by my presence."

"Not at all, Elizabeth. They are in need of all the help they can get. Do come. I know old Mr. Fry would love to have you sit by his chair and read to him. He used to be a schoolmaster, but his sight is so poor, he cannot see to read anymore. We just started a new book of sermons. While you continue with that, I can visit Mrs. Turpin and her little boy."

"Very well, Mother. Let me go up and get my cloak."

After a quick introduction to the blind Mr. Fry, Elizabeth said good-bye to her mother and took out her book.

"More sermons, eh?" said the elderly man.

"That is what my mother said you were reading together. Would you prefer something else?"

He peered at her through thick spectacles and said,

"Anything else. I have some books over there. I have read them all before, but at least I will be able to stay awake."

Elizabeth choked on her laughter, and he said, "I am sorry if I have shocked you. Please do not tell your mother. She has a very kind heart, and I would hate to disappoint her."

"No, no, Mr. Fry. I will not tell her anything. Would you perhaps like to hear a more amusing tale?"

"As I said, Lady Elizabeth, anything would be preferable to those dull sermons."

"I happen to have slipped my novel into my cloak pocket. It is a dreadful gothic tale about a damsel in distress and . . ."

"Read away!" said the old man.

"The wind howling through the trees sent a shiver up her spine. In the distance, a dog howled, too. Marie pulled up the hood on her coat and dug in her heels. The stallion leaped forward . . ."

Two hours later, her mother entered the room. Neither Mr. Fry nor Elizabeth noticed her presence until Mrs. Lightfoot gasped.

"Elizabeth! What are you reading? That is certainly not the book of sermons I gave you."

Before she could speak, Mr. Fry said, "I hope you will not blame your daughter, madam. I received this novel in the post yesterday from my cousin in Bath. I wanted to read it so that I could properly thank her. Your daughter was obliging enough to do so for me."

Mrs. Lightfoot gave a tight little smile and said, "Oh, well, I suppose that is all right then. Very well, but we should be going."

"I don't mind staying, Mother, if Mr. Fry is not too tired."

"I would greatly appreciate it, Mrs. Lightfoot," said the retired schoolmaster.

"I don't know." She thought a moment and then

asked, "You will have no difficulty finding your way back home?"

"I will send the maid with her," said the gentleman.

"Thank you. Then I will bid you good day, Mr. Fry. Do not be late for supper, Elizabeth. You know how your father feels about tardiness."

"Yes, Mother. Good-bye."

When the door closed again, Elizabeth giggled, and Mr. Fry said, "Shh, my lady. She might hear."

After a moment, Elizabeth said, "You are very kind to take the blame, Mr. Fry, and a very quick study."

"I would never have been able to survive the pranks of naughty schoolboys had I not been quick. And I wanted to pay you back for bringing such an entertaining novel my way."

"If you like novels, I have many of them that I have finished. I could send them to you. Oh," she began. "I am sorry. I do not think my mother would read them to you."

"Never mind. I shall simply enjoy this one. Now, we are wasting time. Read on, MacDuff," he quipped.

"Good evening, Elizabeth," said Steven Lightfoot.

His stepdaughter smiled and said, "Good evening, Mr. Lightfoot. I hope you are well."

"Very well, thank you. And you?"

"I am fine." Fishing for some further innocuous comment, she added, "Are you ready for the spring planting?"

"Yes, yes, we have all our plans made, the seeds are ready. All we need do is wait for the good Lord to bring us warmer weather."

Elizabeth smiled. This was one topic she could open without fear of her stepfather sermonizing. If he was nothing else, Steven Lightfoot was an excellent farmer, and he managed his estate well. His tenants, though not wealthy, were well-housed and well-fed.

"I have some new seeds for a superior strain of peas

that I plan to try this year. I will give you some to take to your grandfather. I know he enjoys trying new species on the home farm."

"That is very kind of you, sir," replied Elizabeth.

He waved away this compliment and said, "Your mother told me you spent the afternoon reading to Mr. Fry. I am pleased to see that you do sometimes think of others more than yourself."

Elizabeth could feel her hackles rising at his condescending comments. How could he say such things to her? She refrained from retorting that she was not some frivolous Society miss, however. It would only make him preach at her.

Her voice was clipped as she replied, "Mr. Fry is a very nice man. I was pleased to help."

"Yes, but I understand that he asked you to read some novel that his cousin had sent to him. I do hope you will not allow the tone of the work to creep into your language or behavior."

Elizabeth bit her tongue. After taking a deep breath, she said, "I would not dream of doing so. It is merely a sort of fairy tale. I appreciate your concern, but I do think, at my age, that my character is formed well enough that reading this novel will not impair my judgment."

"Good, good. Ah, here is your mother. Shall we go in to dinner?"

He rose and led the way to the dining room. When they were all seated and the attending servants had their heads bowed, too, Mr. Lightfoot led them in a five-minute prayer.

"Amen," said everyone.

Elizabeth lifted the spoonful of cold soup to her lips. Perhaps she *was* a little spoiled. She greatly preferred her meals to be warm at the very least.

* * *

For the next two days, Elizabeth went to Mr. Fry's house after breakfast and read to him. After completing the novel, she read poetry, another of his favorites.

When she was putting on her cloak on Thursday, he said, "I will miss you, my lady. I hope it has not been so very dull, entertaining an old man."

"Certainly not! I have enjoyed myself immensely, Mr. Fry. And I have a surprise for you."

"A surprise?" he asked, peering at her through those thick spectacles.

"Yes, I found a young lad to come over several times a week to read to you."

"How kind of you," he said. "Who is it?"

"The village innkeeper's nephew."

"I didn't know he had a nephew. He certainly never attended the village school."

"No, he is from London. He has a chance to work in a barrister's office, but he needs polishing. I thought you could help him, and he can read to you. What do you think?"

"It might work," said the old man.

"Good. I told him to come by in the morning. And I will not forget to send you those novels."

"Thank you, Lady Elizabeth. You are very kind to put yourself out like this."

"I have enjoyed myself, too. And thank you again for saving me from the inevitable parental lecture. My mother would have felt obliged to tell my stepfather, and, well, that would not have been pleasant. Take care, Mr. Fry. I will certainly stop in the next time I visit."

"Good-bye, my lady."

Elizabeth went out of the cottage with a smile on her face. Her stepfather's words came floating back to her and she frowned. No, she was not like most of the *ton,* who thought only of themselves, fashion, and parties. She often thought of others.

Elizabeth climbed into the dogcart and breathed a sigh of relief as she put aside these silly ideas.

Elizabeth sat through dinner with her mother and stepfather, saying very little. When they left Mr. Lightfoot to his port, she knew she had to speak to her mother about her half brother. The time had come.

She put off the inevitable, trailing after her mother while trying to think of a way to broach the topic. In the drawing room, her mother was already pulling gold thread in and out of a linen cloth, her fingers moving deftly.

Holding up the finished cross with pride, her mother said, "There you are, Elizabeth. What do you think?"

Elizabeth touched the shiny thread and said, "It is beautiful, Mother. I wish I were half as good with a needle."

"You could be if you had the patience to practice. I must admit, I do get a great deal of satisfaction from my needlework."

"You should come to London, Mother, and visit the drapers. They bring in threads and cloth from all over the world, you know."

"Oh, I don't need such folderol as that. The village shops have everything I need. This thread was special, of course, since it was for the altar cloth. Your stepfather sent all the way to York for it."

"But, Mother, don't you ever long to see the shops again? You haven't been to London in years!"

"Because I do not need to go," came the sensible reply.

"Don't you want to see Val?" asked Elizabeth.

She saw the shadow of pain in those green eyes before her mother bowed her head.

Taking her mother's hands in hers, Elizabeth said, "Mother, you should come to London with me. Come for a month. Talk to Val. I know you miss him."

"I cannot," whispered her mother, shaking her hands

free. "I cannot condone what Val has done. He has chosen to defy your father."

"Stepfather," said Elizabeth, endowing the word with scorn.

"Elizabeth, you should not speak in that tone about . . ."

"Steven Lightfoot means nothing to me, Mother! No, that is not true. He means that I have lost not only my brother, but my mother as well!"

"Elizabeth! Stop!"

"Why? Does your religion not allow the truth? The truth is that your husband, Val's own father, forces your son to live in the most appalling conditions just because Val does not wish to live like a religious martyr!"

"Enough, young lady! Go to your room!" yelled her stepfather, throwing out his arm and pointing toward the door. "Enough of your blasphemies in this house! Leave your mother alone."

"Mother," whispered Elizabeth.

Her mother only shook her head.

Elizabeth stood and walked regally to the door. When she was beside her stepfather, she said calmly, "I will leave in the morning, if that is all right, sir."

"Very well. I will not deny you shelter for the night, but I think it best if you keep to your room."

Elizabeth nodded and left the drawing room. As she walked toward the stairs, she heard the door close and voices rose. Her mother was crying.

Elizabeth thought she would never sleep that night, but her fatigue was such that she finally found release. Her dreams were troubled, however, and she rose early, her eyes burning.

Her maid crept in and helped her dress.

"We'll be leaving as soon as the carriage comes around, won't we, my lady?"

"Yes, why?"

"Oh, these servants think they are so much better than me with their religious ways. I'll be glad to go home."

"Me, too," said Elizabeth.

Glancing toward the door, she noticed an envelope on the floor.

"Dulcie, what is that?"

The maid retrieved it, and Elizabeth opened it cautiously, as if it might bite. She smiled as she read.

"Is it good news, my lady?"

"Yes. Not the best," she said, thinking that the best news would be that her mother was running away with her, but it was still good news. Elizabeth reread the short missive.

Dear Elizabeth,

Take this letter to your grandmother's solicitors. They are to transfer the small annuity I receive to Val, paying him an allowance from the interest each month. I hope you will not think too badly of me, dearest daughter.

My love always,
Your Mother

Elizabeth's eyes filled, but her smile allayed her maid's concern. She dashed away the tears and said, "Come on. We will leave now and find something to eat at the inn."

Gideon swung his leg over the horse's broad back and nodded to the groom, who released the big gelding's head.

"Have a good trip, Captain," called Lady Louisa from the bottom step, where she stood with the countess.

"Thank you. I will see you in London. Lady Rotherford, you will see to it that Lord Winters leaves today, won't you?"

"Never fear. I'll have the silly boy in the carriage in an hour, green-gilled or not. Take care, Captain."

Gideon grinned and waved as he kicked the horse's

sides. Within ten minutes, he was on the road, a great weight lifted from his shoulders.

While he appreciated the hospitality of Wintersford, Gideon was glad to be getting under way with the great scheme, as he had come to think of it. He was most anxious to make the acquaintance of his intended.

Gideon had heard enough of Elizabeth's likes and dislikes. He knew her favorite color was green, her favorite food was roasted pheasant, and that she disliked strawberries. Her birthday was the first of May, only a month away, and she would be seven and twenty. He smiled, wondering if by that date he would be in a position to offer her a gift. He made a mental note to save some of the money in his purse to purchase something for her, something with an emerald—her favorite jewel.

Since Avery, Lord Winters, had drunk too much and risen with a sore head, he had elected to ride with the servants and the luggage. Gideon could not bear the thought of traveling all the way to London in a carriage, but because the vehicle would leave later and not arrive until the next day, he was forced to stop for the night, too. They had agreed to meet at the White Horse in Beaconsfield. It was a small inn, but according to Lord Winters, they served an excellent ale.

Gideon arrived just before five o'clock and was shown the rooms they had bespoken.

The innkeeper, a garrulous fellow, confided that they were expecting a huge crowd in the next hour or two, as soon as the prizefight in the neighboring village was over.

He rubbed his hands together and said, "We're full to the rafters tonight!"

"Good for business, I suppose," said Gideon. "It will be noisy, though."

The innkeeper said hastily, "That's why I put you and his lordship in the two rooms at the back. Less noise that way."

"Good man," said Gideon. "Now, until the mayhem breaks loose, I understand you have an excellent ale."

"Th' best in three counties, sir."

"Good. I'd like a glass of your best."

"In the private parlor?"

"No, the taproom will be fine for me. I will be down in a few minutes."

As Gideon descended the stairs, he realized that the innkeeper's prediction of an hour or two was off the mark. Loud voices rang out from the common room as toast after toast was proposed. He toyed with the idea of changing to the private parlor, but on reflection, he decided that he was becoming too accustomed to rubbing shoulders only with the privileged. An afternoon of rowdy companionship would do him good.

When the innkeeper brought the second glass of ale to his table, Gideon said, "You live up to your reputation, sir. This is the best ale I have ever tasted."

"Thank you, sir," said the man, flushing with pride. Someone yelled an obscenity in response to a proposed wager, and the innkeeper leaned close. "There is a little problem, sir. I was hoping you might be willing to help me with it."

"I will try," shouted Gideon over the noise. He motioned toward the hall. When they were outside the taproom, he said, "What is it?"

"A young lady has arrived, seeking a room—the sort of young lady a man in my position doesn't like to deny."

"I see. And how can I help?"

"I was wondering, sir, if you and his lordship might stay in the same room. I will have another bed brought in."

"I don't see why not," said Gideon. "Tell the young lady she is welcome to my room. I will go upstairs and move my things."

"As to that, sir, she is already in the room. I daren't let her stay out here unprotected."

"She is traveling alone?"

"Oh, no sir. She has outriders and a maid, but no man to look after her, and I didn't wish to tell her to remain in her carriage."

"Of course not. Then I will go and fetch my things."

"I told the maid to pack them up and place them in the hall. I will put them in his lordship's room."

"Very well," said Gideon.

"You're very kind to take this so well. Thank you, Mr. Sparks."

Gideon started to correct him, to tell him he was Captain Sparks, then he stopped. Perhaps he should quit telling people he was a captain. How could one be a captain without a ship? On this gloomy thought, Gideon followed the innkeeper up the narrow stairs to see that all his belongings had been placed in the other room.

He listened as the innkeeper knocked on the door to his old room and said, "Excuse me, my lady, but the gentleman has agreed to give up his room."

"That's very good of him. You will thank him for me, will you not?" came the soft reply.

"Certainly," said the innkeeper. "And I will have your supper served in the private parlor as soon as possible."

Gideon heard the door close. He was suddenly very tired, and he entered the room and lay down on the bed. A moment later, there was a knock, and two young men entered with another bed. A maid followed with bed linens and quickly made up the extra bed.

Gideon thought that if he were kind, he would take the other bed and leave the softer one for Lord Winters. *Devil take him,* he thought. He shouldn't have drunk so heavily the night before and had to ride in the carriage.

Gideon closed his eyes. The innkeeper was right about one thing. The room was quiet. He couldn't even hear the commotion in the taproom.

Then he heard the sound of someone singing—the young lady next door. He smiled. It was a pleasant, lilting voice.

Early one morning, just as the sun was rising . . .

Where had he heard that lately? Oh yes. Lady Louisa had been singing the same tune in her garden.

The words penetrated the wall, clear and true.

I saw a young maiden in the valley far below
How can you lie to me,
I, who would die for ye,
How can you do a poor maiden so?

Gideon sat up, frowning in amazement. Those were not the correct words. He was certain of that. But how could some young lady be singing the same song with the same incorrect lyrics as Lady Louisa?

The singing stopped, and he heard the maid enter next door. The walls were paper thin. He could practically hear the two women breathing.

"Supper is all laid out, my lady. Shall I accompany you downstairs?"

Gideon hurried to the door and cracked it open.

The young lady was saying, "No, I will be fine, Dulcie. But don't worry. I will tell the innkeeper to keep the parlor door latched. I noticed all the carriages and excellent horseflesh in the yard. Half of London's Corinthian set must be here tonight."

And there she was, turning to close the door. She glanced up, and he saw those wonderful green eyes, the same eyes from the painting, with the same sparkling vitality.

He closed the door quickly. Had she seen him? Had she seen him staring like a looby? And if she had, had the door been open enough that she would recognize him the next time she saw him?

Why the devil hadn't the innkeeper told him that it was Lady Elizabeth Winters? Never mind, he thought. Here was the perfect opportunity to meet her without all the dazzle of London! He would just go downstairs . . .

No, she would think him one of the men who had descended on the inn after watching the prizefight.

Gideon snapped his fingers. He would have the innkeeper tell her that the man who had given up his room wanted someplace quiet to eat his supper and would she mind sharing the private parlor?

He frowned. He could just imagine what the countess would say about that! A gentleman would never play so loose with a lady's reputation! Dining in private with a perfect stranger? Never would a lady do such a thing!

Devil take the blasted countess, he thought. Did she, or did she not, want him to wed her granddaughter? Still, if dining with her in a private parlor in a country inn would compromise Elizabeth, he didn't dare make the request.

But he had to see her, to get a good look at her.

Just then, the door opened, and the two burly stable lads who had brought the extra bed entered, carrying the moaning Lord Winters.

"What's the matter with his lordship?" demanded Gideon, the interruption of his plotting irritating him in the extreme. Mallard and Grimes, Winters' valet, followed closely.

While Grimes attended to his master's comfort—Gideon noticed he had automatically placed Winters on the better bed—Mallard said, "I am afraid that it was not the drink that made Lord Winters ill. It is some ailment. Hopefully it will pass quickly, but I was most distressed when the landlord said that you and his lordship were sharing a room. I fear the sickness may be catching, Captain."

"I am never ill." Gideon winced as a bucket was placed in front of Winters, and the viscount retched. "Still, I think I will go downstairs if you two can manage."

"Certainly, sir."

Gideon closed the door softly. Downstairs, outside the private parlor, he hesitated. Raucous laughter emanated from the taproom down the hall, and he shook his head, unwilling to face such disorder. He would simply have to beg the lady's forgiveness for barging in.

Still Gideon hesitated. Lady Rotherford had warned him time and again that a gentleman always kept in mind the reputation of his lady. He would never do anything to compromise her.

With a curse, Gideon went for a stroll in the yard, but the night was chilly and damp. He wandered into the taproom and had a glass of ale. Finally, he could stand it no longer, and he returned to the hall outside the private parlor.

Gideon pushed on the door, but it was latched from the inside. He knocked. A moment later, Elizabeth opened the door.

"Yes?"

Thinking how foolish it was of her to open the door without first asking who was there, he said, "You should not open the door, my lady. It could have been anyone."

She frowned up at him. "And so it was, but you look very familiar."

Then her face cleared and she smiled, opening the door wider to allow him to enter. Gideon stepped inside but remained by the door.

"I am sorry, my lady. I should have introduced myself. I am next door to you upstairs."

"Yes, you are the gentleman who gave up his room. It was very gallant of you, sir. Would you like to join me?" she asked, still smiling in the friendliest manner.

"A pleasure to be of service, my lady. First, I want to introduce myself. My name is Gideon Sparks. I was the captain of the ship that went down with your cousin on board."

"Captain Sparks?" said Elizabeth. She took his large hand between hers and shook it warmly. Closing the door behind them, she drew him toward the table.

"How good it is to meet you! My grandmother has had

nothing but praise for you in her letters! She has painted quite a heroic picture, I can tell you. Come in. Do sit down, and tell me what brings you to this particular inn." Sitting down, she gestured to the chair next to hers.

Gideon remained standing. "Not the prizefight, I assure you. If Lord Winters and I had known . . ."

"Avery is here, too? Where is he? I have not seen him since he returned to England, since his near brush with death!" She made as if to rise, and he stayed her with a hand.

"Your cousin is unwell, my lady."

"Unwell? I must go to him."

"I would not advise it. His valet—and mine, too, for that matter—are with him. His stomach is . . . upset. He will be fine in a day or two."

"But to have only servants looking after him when he is ill. I will go to him," said Elizabeth.

Gideon felt his heart soar. Not only was she a beauty, but she was compassionate, too. He waved aside her offer and said, "There is really no need, my lady. I will be checking on him. He arrived only a few minutes ago and is now getting settled. Mallard said he feared it might be catching."

"Oh, well, in that case." Her eyes danced as she said, "I must confess that when someone has contracted the *mal à l'estomac,* I try to avoid all contact with them." Wrinkling her nose, she added, "Not a pleasant sort of illness."

"Indeed not," said Gideon. He marveled at her beauty and wit. She was just as he had hoped—clever, compassionate, and friendly.

She patted the chair next to her and said, "But won't you be seated and have some wine? I will have the landlord bring another glass."

Gideon looked into those green eyes, just as he had so many times before, and he was torn—torn with the desire to remain by her side and the desire to do the proper thing. Lady Rotherford had assured him that the only way to win a lady was to do what was right and proper.

He and Lady Elizabeth, not being related, could not remain alone in the private parlor. He was unwilling to go upstairs and sit in the room with the ailing viscount. He simply had to ask her if she might be willing to return to her room as soon as she had finished eating her supper.

"No, thank you. I really should not, but . . ."

"What is it, Captain?"

"It is rather awkward, but I find myself without a place to rest, what with Lord Winters upstairs and the crowd in the taproom. I cannot very well remain here with you." When she didn't respond, he added, "I would not wish to compromise you. I mean, neither of us wants that!"

She blinked at this, and then said, "No, certainly not."

Elizabeth lowered her head as if thinking, while Gideon waited anxiously. What would she say? Would she thank him for his thoughtfulness?

When she raised her face to his again, however, the sparkle in her eyes was not amusement, but anger. Was she angry with him? What the deuce had he said to make her angry? All he was trying to do was protect her blessed reputation. He tried again.

"I thought perhaps while you finish your supper, I will wait in the hall. Afterward, you can go up to your room, and I will make myself comfortable in that chair by the fire."

"How very wise you are, Captain. As a matter of fact, I am already finished. You may have the parlor." Her tone was flat and lifeless, but infinitely polite.

Gideon glanced at the half-empty plate and protested.

"Not at all," she responded. "I will bid you good night. I shall also say good-bye. I will probably be gone before you and Avery rise in the morning."

She patted her lips with the serviette and rose. The look of disdain—there could be no mistaking that—made him reach out to stop her, but she shook her head.

"Eliza . . . Lady Elizabeth," he said.

The look she gave him would have frozen fire. Oh, he thought, she might have Lady Louisa's eyes, but this expression was the countess all over again.

"Good night, Captain Sparks."

"Good night, my lady," was all he could say.

When the door had closed, he let out a string of curses that would have made the most hardened sailor blush.

The door opened slightly, and she said, "Did you say something, Captain?"

"No, no. Good night."

With a regal nod, she closed the door.

This time his curses were silent, but the passion was just as real.

Elizabeth stalked up the stairs to her room. Her maid, who was eating her own supper, put down her fork.

"Oh, go ahead and finish your supper, Dulcie. One of us might as well eat tonight!" said Elizabeth, plopping down on the bed.

"Whatever is the matter, my lady?"

"I have just met the most dreadful man! So insulting!"

"Shall I get your cousin? I just learned that Lord Winters is staying here tonight, too. Isn't that a coincidence?"

"Veritable serendipity," said Elizabeth flatly as she began to remove her clothes. When the maid set aside her dinner, she added, "I can manage by myself, Dulcie. Finish your dinner."

"I couldn't, my lady. Not knowing that you are starving."

"I am hardly starving. I managed to down enough to sustain me before *he* came into the parlor."

"I knew I should have gone down with you. One of those men from the prizefight?"

"Prizefight? Heavens, no! This is the man who is traveling with my cousin. Actually, I met him, after a fashion, in the stables at Wintersford." She realized the maid was looking at her strangely and said, "But never mind about that. The point is, my cousin is ill. The captain doesn't want to catch it, and so, pretty as you please, he commandeers my private parlor, so that he may have a refuge!"

"Wouldn't he let you stay to finish your supper?"

"No! He didn't want to compromise me, he said. More like he didn't want to have to wed me. Ooh, I would so like to tell him that I wouldn't marry him if he were the last man on earth. That's what I should have said!"

Elizabeth shrugged out of her dress and into a wrapper. After sitting down on the bed cross-legged, she asked, "Why is it that men are such beasts? And not just beasts. They are dim-witted, too! They are so busy worrying about what Society will say that they lose all good sense! Anyone with half a brain would have said, 'Pardon me, my lady, but under these extraordinary circumstances, I think it would be permissible for the two of us to share the parlor'! What would have been wrong with that?"

"Nothing that I can see," ventured the maid.

"Exactly! You see it. I see it. But can a man see it? No, he is too afraid of being trapped in parson's mousetrap to use good common sense! This Captain Sparks has probably lost his common sense through a lack of usage!" she added for good measure.

"I'll just take this tray downstairs, my lady. Can I bring you anything?"

"What? Oh, no thank you, Dulcie. I really did have enough to eat."

Alone, Elizabeth lay back on the bed and stared at the ceiling. She closed her eyes and recalled the unpleasant episode.

Not that it had been entirely unpleasant. It hadn't been unpleasant before he started talking nonsense. Before that, she had been eager to share the parlor with him, to get to know the American she had met in the stable while playing the part of a groom.

When she first opened the parlor door, she had merely been conscious of broad shoulders, a tall, trim figure, and a handsome face. That nose of his, so straight and strong. And the jaw. She always admired a man with a firm jaw. His hair was quite dark, something she had not been able to see in the shadows of the stable at Wintersford, and his smile—until he had started spouting folderol—was quite captivating.

The captain and Avery must have been visiting Wintersford all the while she was gone to her mother's house.

With a start, Elizabeth chided herself. How quickly she forgot that he had insulted her with his foolish proprieties! If only she had not angered her stepfather and had left a day later! She would not then have been exposed to the insulting Captain Sparks.

If only there had not been a prizefight to make the inn so crowded.

A pouting frown wrinkled her brow.

If only I had stayed home and met him properly.

Chapter Six

Gideon spent an uncomfortable night in the chair. Though he was warm enough, he had a crick in his neck and his legs were cramped. The revelers from the prize-fight had finally settled down around dawn. He longed for the road, where he could get into the saddle and work out the stiffness.

He was not completely displeased with the turn of events. He had finally met his Elizabeth—for so he had begun to think of her. He was pleased that he had behaved in a gentlemanly fashion. Had he not, he might have frightened her away. Certainly, he had wanted to while away the evening in her company, getting to know her better, but that would come later. At least he had managed to not give her a disgust of him.

The innkeeper entered and asked, "Would you like your breakfast served in here, Captain? His lordship has already eaten his gruel up in the room."

"That will be fine," said Gideon. Before the innkeeper could close the door, he asked, "And what of Lady Elizabeth?"

"Her ladyship has already left, sir. She's been gone this hour and more."

"I see. Thank you."

Gideon frowned. That was very rude of her to leave without speaking to her cousin. She should at least have had the decency to do that—unless, of course, she was afraid of encountering *him.*

Surely that couldn't be. He knew she had been a bit miffed at being sent away, but the countess had assured him that any young lady valued her reputation above all else, and thus would equally value a man who respected her reputation.

Could the countess have been wrong?

The door opened again, and he looked up to find the viscount sagging against the frame. After a deep breath, Winters entered and took the first chair he encountered.

Gideon grinned and said, "You look ghastly."

"Thank you. I am aware of that. But at least the room is not spinning. Egad! What a rough day and night!"

"But you are feeling better?"

"I am well enough to travel—slowly."

"Good. Did you know that your cousin was here last night?"

"Yes, she stopped in to speak to me this morning. What the devil did you do to her?" asked the viscount.

His brows came together, and Gideon said, "Do to . . . I didn't do anything to the wench! What did she tell you?"

"Tell me? Nothing, but when I mentioned your name, her face turned all prissy and haughty. She told me she had already had the pleasure, and from the way she said *pleasure,* I can assure you she did not take any pleasure from the encounter."

"The devil you say! Hellfire and . . . blast that grandmother of yours!"

"Grandmother?" said the viscount, his green pallor lifting as he grinned.

"Yes, it's all her fault. She told me that under no circumstances should I put myself forward or make your cousin uncomfortable. She said I should treat Elizabeth like a delicate flower. Bah!"

"Elizabeth? A delicate flower? What rubbish! The girl has eaten more seasoned men than you for breakfast! I thought you realized that!"

"Why the devil would I think that? Oh, I'll admit that

Lady Louisa seemed to think Elizabeth would be able to handle herself, but it was the countess who insisted that I treat your cousin with kid gloves. I thought the wench had been hurt or wounded in love."

"Not Elizabeth! I doubt she has ever even imagined herself in love. I am sorry, old boy. I can see that I should have had more of a hand in your training as a Society beau, not just the exterior—the clothes, the boots, and the amusements."

Gideon dropped into the chair across the table from his friend and said glumly, "So I have already ruined my chances with the fair Elizabeth."

"Take heart, man. To remedy the situation, the next time you meet, you must behave in the coldest manner to her. That should intrigue her."

"I rather favor acting in the warmest manner. That might show her that I wouldn't mind compromising her in the least."

"Hm. You will simply have to play it by ear. In my knowledge of her former suitors, they have all been singularly enamored of her. It seems to have had the opposite effect to what you might imagine. But then, I am only her cousin."

"Exactly how many suitors have offered for her?"

"Oh, it's hard to say. They usually ask permission from Grandfather, not me."

"Five?" Gideon's eyes widened as the viscount cocked his head upward. "Ten?" Again that movement. "Good God, Winters!"

"Good God, indeed," said the viscount with a laugh.

"She has turned down more than ten suitors," murmured Gideon. With a perplexed frown, he demanded, "What the devil makes you think that she might find me acceptable?"

"I thought she might because you are different. Then my grandmother got hold of you. Now . . ."

Gideon muttered a curse as the landlord entered with

a tray. The viscount took one look at the kidney pie and steaming prunes and clambered to his feet.

Hurrying from the room, he said over his shoulder, "I will be upstairs. When you are done with your breakfast, we will head for London."

"Nothing for you?" called Gideon.

A rude comment floated back as the viscount left the room.

Elizabeth entered her house in Mayfair and dropped her bonnet into her maid's hands, her cloak in the butler's, and her parasol in the footman's hands.

"It is so good to be back, Roberts!"

"And a pleasure it is to have you back, my lady," said the butler with a smile. He was young, almost as young as she, and he possessed a sunny disposition, one of the chief reasons she had hired him. He kept her town house ready for her to drop in at any time, as, indeed, she was known to do.

"Has my grandmother arrived yet?"

"Lady Louisa sent word that she will be arriving tomorrow morning. In the note she sent to me, she enclosed another for you, my lady. I put it on the desk in your room, along with your other invitations."

"Wonderful! I shall just go up and knock off the dust of the road. Will you have Dominick fix a tray of something and send it up?"

"Very good, my lady."

Elizabeth followed her maid and luggage up the narrow stairs. She had purchased the town house when she had reached her majority at five and twenty. It was not large, but it was big enough for her and her grandmother. The drawing room was quite spacious, a feature that had attracted Elizabeth, since she had numerous callers in the afternoon.

Having given her grandmother the bedroom that

overlooked the quiet garden, Elizabeth's bedroom was in the front of the house. She enjoyed waking to the sound of carriages and the occasional calls of servants as they swept the front steps. It always reminded her that she was in London, and when in London, anything might happen.

While Dulcie set about putting everything away, Elizabeth kicked off her shoes and sat on the bed to read her mail. It was the first of April and already the invitations were pouring in—an alfresco breakfast at the Donovans, a ball in honor of the youngest Miss McKenzie, a rout at the Sinclairs, and several invitations to dinner, cards, and music. When she first arrived, her initial inclination had been to accept all of them. Through the years, however, Elizabeth had learned to be more selective. She sorted the cards into two piles—those she would accept immediately, and those which would require further consideration.

A footman entered with a tray. Elizabeth looked up and smiled. "Good morning, Andrew. I hope your leg has fully healed."

"It's as right as rain, my lady. Thank you for remembering. Will there be anything else?"

"No, that's all. Thank you."

He gave a quick bow and left. Elizabeth got up and padded over to the small table in front of the fire where Andrew had placed the silver tray. Dulcie hurried forward and lifted the dome off the plate.

"Hm, smells wonderful. Dulcie, why don't you finish the unpacking later? You must be famished, too. Go down and see what Dominick has for you."

"Thank you, my lady. I wouldn't mind having a little something. We left the inn so very early this morning."

"I know," said Elizabeth.

She took a bite of the poached salmon and sighed. It was delicious. Dominick was a treasure. Let the rest of London pursue their French chefs. She would not trade her Italian chef for anything. What he could do with a tomato was incredible.

When she had finished her meal, Elizabeth removed her gown and put on a wrapper. Picking up the novel that Dulcie had already placed on the bedside table, she opened to the final chapter. Her eyes soon grew heavy, and she was forced to set it aside. Lying back, she closed her eyes. Dulcie was right. They had risen much too early to escape the inn before the odiously handsome Captain Sparks was about.

She wondered if he had missed her.

Late that evening, after a trip to the theater, Gideon and the viscount arrived at their club for a bite of supper. While waiting for their food, Gideon returned to the topic of his debacle with Elizabeth.

When the viscount dismissed his concern, he said, "Damn it all, Winters, you cannot tell me that you are not in the least concerned for your cousin's reputation."

"I am merely saying that you were no threat to her reputation. Who would have ever known you were there?"

"What about all those men who had come to watch that prizefight? What if they had seen us alone in the parlor?"

"What's done is done. Look, there is Lord Beresford. We met his wife in the park a couple of weeks ago. Do you remember? Ah, good. Here's the food."

While they downed the passable fare, Winters kept up an ongoing monologue, telling Gideon about each of the members who entered. They were mostly young men, and several stopped by and were introduced. Some of them Gideon remembered from his earlier visit to London. Now that he had been clothed by Stulz, however, the young men took more notice of his presence. Two of them, whom he had met previously, evinced no knowledge of their previous introduction.

Lord Hazelton, a tall, slender fellow with a shock of blond hair, pulled up a chair.

After spending a moment on the introductions, he winked at Lord Winters and said, "Have you heard about Wakefield's little society?"

"Society? No, I haven't seen him in over a month."

"Oh, then perhaps I shouldn't . . . a fellow doesn't like to carry tales, especially when it is to a relative of the young lady in question."

Gideon leaned forward and said, "What lady?"

Avery put his hand out and asked casually, "What sort of society is it? Perhaps I would like to join."

Lowering his voice, Lord Hazelton said, "The name of it is quite clever. Sir Landon came up with it himself, so I am told. It is called S.O.R.E.S.—Society of Rejected Elizabethan Suitors. There must be twenty chaps who belong! I wanted to join, but I never did come up to scratch, you know. It is sure to be the talk of the town."

Gideon leaned closer and said quietly, "It had better not be your talk, chap."

Winters chuckled and said, "Do not concern yourself, Captain. People are always making up nonsensical little jokes like this. It is best not to pay any attention to it."

Gideon glared at his friend.

Lord Hazelton glanced at the captain and squeaked, "I certainly didn't mean any harm in it."

"Of course not," said Winters. "It is just a stupid little diversion for Sir Landon. I daresay it will never leave this club."

"Of course not," said the nervous Lord Hazelton, his eyes darting to Gideon and then back to the viscount. He stood up and said, "I must be going. I have to, uh, see someone . . . good-bye."

"Good-bye, Hazelton," said Winters. When they were alone again, the viscount said, "That is not the way to get along in Society, Captain. If you take too great an interest in something, you will find that other people will follow suit. The problem will go away if we do nothing to exacerbate it."

"Ignore it and it will go away? I am not accustomed to such a cowardly way of handling things. At the very least, you will want to tell Elizabeth. She ought to be forewarned."

The viscount shuddered and shook his head. "I am afraid that might be a case of killing the messenger."

"Do you not care that it is your cousin that they are making game of?"

"They? It is probably only Wakefield and one or two others. Sir Landon warned me that he would not take his rejection lying down. I suppose he was serious."

"Does he love her?"

Winters looked pensive. After a moment, he shook his head. "No, but I think he expected her to accept his offer. We all did. Still, he handled it badly. I don't really blame her for rejecting him."

"So perhaps Elizabeth really does have feelings for this Sir Landon," said Gideon.

"Who can say with females? I don't pretend to understand the creatures. Here, have another glass. My grandmother and Lady Louisa will be in London tomorrow. We shall have very little peace after that." He took a deep drink and added, "Thank heavens we have bachelor quarters to escape to. Can you imagine living in the same house with my grandmother?"

Gideon could not help but smile at this. "I admire the countess, but she is rather strong-willed."

"Devilishly," said the viscount. As the servant cleared the table, he said, "The theater tonight, I think."

"Why the theater?" asked Gideon.

"We have to let the ladies see you, my dear Captain. One look at you, and they will be clamoring for introductions. And then we shall have invitations to spare!"

Gideon groaned.

"Needs must, old chap. When they discover there is

new blood, dressed fashionably and well-spoken, they will be throwing their daughters at your head. It will only help Elizabeth notice you."

The viscount rose and headed for the door. Gideon finished the last swallow of his brandy and rose.

He didn't care about any of those daughters. There was only one young lady he wanted to capture, and he very much doubted she ever wanted to see him again.

On this glum thought, Gideon pasted a smile on his face and prepared to meet the dragon-mothers at the theater.

"Penny, I am looking forward to this Season in a way I have not done in several years," said Elizabeth to her friend.

They were sitting on the sofa in the large drawing room of Elizabeth's town house. Lady Louisa, who had arrived that morning not long after Penelope and Roger, was resting in her room. Roger was worn out by the short journey and was also resting. The young ladies, however, were looking through the invitations again.

"Why is that, Elizabeth? Do you think that this year you will find your prince?" asked Penelope.

Elizabeth rolled her eyes at her friend and said, "That would take a miracle. No, silly, it is because I know that I shall enjoy it more with you here."

"I am still not easy with this arrangement. I think you and Roger planned all this behind my back. However, I must admit that it is good to see him out of the house. He looks better, don't you think?"

"Indeed I do," said Elizabeth, smiling at her schoolgirl friend.

She did not add that Penelope appeared livelier, too. It could be the fact that she was dressed in one of Elizabeth's gowns, a cherry red carriage dress that set off her complexion to perfection. Elizabeth had had it made up expressly for Penelope, but she did not tell her friend that, of course. Penelope and Roger were not poor, but they could not afford the expense and luxury of a new wardrobe for the Season. Nor would they like the idea of charity. Still, Elizabeth was determined that she would do all she could to see that Penelope lacked for nothing, even if it meant ordering gowns which she did not personally need and then deciding they suited Penny much better than they did herself. She was not above a little subterfuge in order to get her own way.

"Saturday night is the McKenzies' ball," said Penelope, holding up a stiff white card. "I remember April and May McKenzie at school. Such silly girls! Have they changed much?"

"Not at all, except that they are both married, and to the most boring of men. The ball is for their sister, June. She is a very pretty girl, but she is so clever she may frighten away the gentlemen."

"Yes, I remember at school everyone was always saying how we would be forced to pretend ignorance when in conversation with gentlemen. I am quite glad I did not have to put that to the test for very long. Personally, I think it quite silly. However do you manage?"

Elizabeth grinned and said, "Behold, a spinster."

"Oh, Liz, you are hardly on the shelf."

"Then neither are you, Penny. We are six and twenty, hardly in our dotage. Nor are we silly ninnyhammers. We will be our usual, erudite selves."

"Erudite? No one can accuse either of us of that! I mean, we may read a great deal, but I do not think novels equate to Greek classics," laughed Penelope.

"Can you imagine anything more tedious? Oh, that reminds me. I have not yet told you what came to pass with Val and my mother."

As if mention of her half brother had conjured him, Roberts opened the drawing room door and announced, "Mr. Lightfoot, my lady."

"Val!" said Elizabeth, rising and greeting her brother with a fierce hug. "Come in, do. You will remember Penelope Holloway." She smiled up at him. He was quite tall and slender, and his dark curly hair and bright blue eyes made him a favorite with the ladies.

"What? Oh, yes. Hello, Penny, uh, Miss Holloway. Elizabeth, I must speak to you . . . in private. I know you will excuse us," he said to Penelope, extending his hand to help her rise. In a moment, he and Elizabeth were alone.

"How rude of you, Val. But what is the matter?" She did not add *now,* though the thought crossed her mind. Her half brother lived life scrambling out of one fix and falling into another.

"I needed to see you about . . . you know." When she only frowned, he said, "You know . . . money."

"Of course. I am sorry. I should have sent for you immediately. Mother has relented. She is going to see to it that you have a monthly allowance out of the widow's jointure she received when my father passed away."

"How much?"

"I believe it will be one hundred or so each month."

"Not a great sum," he said. Then he gave her that quick smile of his that had already won him countless hearts at the age of only two and twenty. "I know. Beggars cannot be choosers, and I am grateful to Mother. I know it must have been a very difficult decision. If only she were not so honest, she could then refrain from telling the old skinflint."

"Val," said Elizabeth.

"But he is, Elizabeth. Father is the cheapest man I know. But I will be thankful for the sum Mother has given over to me. It would be better, perhaps, to have paid off my creditors first, but they will simply have to be patient a while longer."

"Val, if you need . . ."

"No, I will not accept a single groat from you, Elizabeth. I shall come about. I always do."

"You'll stay for tea?"

"No, I must be going." He paused at the door and asked, "When will it be arranged? The money, I mean."

"I saw the solicitor this morning. He said he would draw up a draft today and send it around to your lodgings."

"Heavens! I must certainly be going! Good fortune awaits!" With this, Val blew her a kiss and headed out the door.

The day was chilly, but the sun peeked out from behind the clouds with enough regularity that Society saw fit to show itself in the park at the fashionable hour. Elizabeth and Penelope were there, riding in an open carriage with their parasols unfurled. Penny's was the same cherry red as her gown. With her dark hair, she looked quite fetching. Elizabeth wore a bottle green gown with a cream colored pelisse. Her parasol was a gay silk print.

Their progress was very slow because of all the people who stopped to speak to them—not just the gentlemen, but the ladies, too. The cream of London Society seemed to have emerged from its winter cocoon all at once. Penelope might have been secreted in the country for the past few years, but Society had not forgotten her completely. As she flushed with pleasure, the years faded away, and she was a girl again.

When they were alone for a few minutes, Elizabeth asked, "Are you glad you came?"

"Oh, yes, Liz. It is most gratifying that my friends have not forgotten me."

"Of course they remember you!" said Elizabeth. "Oh, look, here is Avery. You probably will not even recognize him."

"Oh, I would know him anywhere," said Penelope. "I

mean, he has not changed one jot. Who is that with him?"

"Gideon Sparks, the man who saved his life." In a fit of pique, she added, "And a more prosy man you will never meet."

Her friend gave her a quizzical look, but said nothing. Avery and Gideon pulled up their horses and doffed their hats.

"Good afteroon, Coz," said Avery.

"Good afternoon," she replied. "You will remember Penelope Holloway."

"Of course. A pleasure to see you again, Miss Holloway. May I present my friend, Captain Sparks?"

"How do you do, Captain," said Penelope.

"A pleasure to meet you, Miss Holloway."

She cocked her head to one side and said, "You are not English, Captain."

"No, Captain Sparks is from America," said Avery.

"Gideon Sparks," whispered Penelope, all color draining from her face. "Captain Gideon Sparks."

"How are you, Lady Elizabeth?" Gideon, who had hardly taken his eyes from Elizabeth, was intent on making her notice him.

Glancing away, she said airily, "I am quite well, Captain. Now, if you will excuse us."

"Miss Holloway, are you all right?" asked the viscount, suddenly noticing Elizabeth's friend. "You appear to have suffered a shock."

"What? No, I . . . that is, I am fine," she said softly. "Fine. Elizabeth, we should not keep the horses standing, should we?"

"Of course, drive on. Good afternoon, gentlemen."

When they were out of earshot, Elizabeth said, "What an odious man. He hardly noticed me at all. I might as well have been invisible. You see why I barely tolerate the man, Penelope. Penny? Whatever is the matter?"

Elizabeth lifted her friend's wrist and chafed it. Penelope looked at her hand as if staring at something of great interest.

"What is the matter? Are you ill? Mr. Cochran, turn the carriage around."

"No, no," said Penny, shaking her head. "There is no need for that."

"But, Penny, you look as if you have seen a ghost."

"I very nearly did," she whispered. Then she burst into tears.

"Take us home at once, Mr. Cochran."

Elizabeth soothed her friend as they traveled the short distance back to Mayfair. Penny would stop crying for a moment, but when she tried to explain her unusual behavior, she would start crying all over again.

When they arrived at home, Elizabeth led her silent friend upstairs and sat her down in the chair before the fireplace.

She dragged another chair forward and took Penny's hands in hers. "Now, tell me what has you so overwrought. If it can be fixed, I will fix it."

"I feel so silly. It is just a name, just a man, but somehow, it makes it seem like it is all happening again, from the start."

"What is happening?"

"Roger. When he was injured, wounded. It was during the last war with the United States, you remember."

"Yes, of course. He was an officer on board a ship and it sank in battle."

"That's right. They had stopped an American ship for something. I don't know. Supplies, or something. Then another ship appeared. Roger told me about it. I can see it all so clearly in my mind."

"But that was four years ago, Penny."

"I know, and I never think of it now. But when I heard that man's name . . ."

"What man?"

"Captain Sparks." Penelope lifted her face to Elizabeth and whispered, "Captain Gideon Sparks was the man who almost killed my brother."

"No! Surely not!"

"Yes, it was he. He fired on Roger's ship and one of the cannonballs, one of Captain Sparks' cannonballs . . ." She shuddered and covered her face. "That is when Roger lost his leg."

"Oh, Penny, I am sorry. No wonder you looked so stricken."

Penelope shook her head and said, "I used to dream about him. I had never seen him, of course, but I would dream about watching him suffer the agonies that Roger has suffered."

"But, Penny, we were at war."

"Yes, yes. I know."

There was a knock on the door and Elizabeth went to answer it.

Andrew, the footman, said, "Sorry to disturb you, my lady, but Mr. Holloway saw his sister crying and wonders if he can have a word with her."

"What? Oh, I . . ."

Penny stood up and smoothed her skirt. "Please tell my brother I will be with him in a few minutes, Andrew."

"Very good, Miss."

Penny busied herself at the washstand, splashing water on her face.

"I'll go down with you," said Elizabeth.

"No, I think it would be best if I speak to him alone."

"Are you going to tell him?"

"Yes, I think he should know. He was on board the captain's ship for a week before they transferred him to a passing freighter that was heading back to England. He might see him on the street. It wouldn't do for him to be caught unawares."

* * *

"Hello, Avery. Didn't know you were back in town," said Valentine Lightfoot.

"Val," said Avery, looking up at the tall young man. "Care for a drink?"

"Thought you'd never ask," said Val, sitting down in a chair and grinning at the viscount and Gideon. "You must be Captain Sparks, the man who has all the ladies swooning."

"I don't know about the last part, but I am Gideon Sparks. And you are?"

"Oh, sorry," said Avery. "This is my . . . what are we to each other, precisely?"

"Not a demmed thing, far as I can tell. I am merely your cousin's half brother."

"Yes, well, this is Elizabeth's brother, Valentine Lightfoot."

"My pleasure, Mr. Lightfoot."

"Call me Val. Everyone does, even the ladies. It makes them feel wicked to call me by my given name." The young man grinned in the most disarming fashion and downed the glass of brandy the viscount handed him.

"Elizabeth's in town," said Avery. "Have you seen her?"

"Saw her yesterday, as a matter of fact. She's back again for another try, I suppose. Don't know why she can't seem to settle on anyone. Not a good thing, I can tell you."

"What we think really doesn't matter, does it?"

"Not a jot!" said the young man cheerfully. "I have gotten wind of a rather amusing new club. Wakefield is behind it, of course. Damn, but I'm glad she had the good sense to turn down that pompous twit! Egad! What a frightful bore he is!"

Gideon smiled at this and said, "You are rather blunt, Mr. Lightfoot."

"Val."

"Val," said Gideon. "So you wouldn't like Wakefield for a brother-in-law?"

"Devil a bit! As to that, if Elizabeth liked him, then that would be it, wouldn't it? I'm just saying that I think she shows rare good sense not to like the fellow. You mark my words, he'll die of the French disease."

"And you won't, the way you carry on with the ladies?" asked Avery with a laugh.

"No, no. The English disease, perhaps," he said with a grin. "After all, my *friends* are all English."

"I don't see how you manage it, Val. You stay one step in front of Bow Street with your scarcely veiled blackmail and one step in front of jealous husbands. How the devil do you do it?"

"Just lucky and clever. Never bite off more than you can, uh, chew, so to speak. Ah, that reminds me. I have an appointment with Lady . . . but I won't carry tales. A pleasure meeting you, Captain."

"And you, Val," said Gideon.

His eyes twinkling with mischief, Val added, "Has my sister met you, Captain? You might be just the type of fellow to rouse her interests. But who knows? Evening." With this cryptic remark, he sauntered out of the room.

"Impudent boy," said Gideon, but he was smiling. "What is this business about blackmail?"

"Oh, he has a network of spies, servants mostly. They tell him about secrets and scandals. He mentions them to the appropriate people and they pay him off to keep him quiet."

"Charming," said Gideon.

"The thing is, everyone knows he's got one foot in debtor's prison, and he is so well-liked that they don't mind paying him. It's never much. Then the scandal breaks and the news is out anyway. He is rather like a living gossip column, that's all."

"Sounds dodgy to me," said Gideon.

"Perhaps, but he's usually right about things, too. Almost like he has a sixth sense about people. He's always there to give a fellow advice on a horse race or at a prize-fight."

"And you say he is Elizabeth's half brother?"

"Yes, his father, Elizabeth's stepfather, is a skinflint. Without Val's little games, he would starve." Avery rose and said, "What say we go to the Sinclairs' rout?"

Rising, Gideon asked, "What exactly is a rout?"

"A boring reception where one fights one's way to the host and hostess, exchanges a few commonplace remarks, and then fights one's way out again. It is, however, a terrific place to meet the crème de la crème."

"Oh, then we should definitely go. I will fit right in," said Gideon.

Fifteen minutes later, they were just entering the elegant town house of the Sinclairs. The hall was crowded, the stairs were crowded, and the drawing room packed. Gideon thought he must have met the whole of London Society by the time they reached their host and hostess, but he continued to field introductions as they retreated.

"There she is," hissed Avery over his shoulder. "Aim in that direction."

Gideon didn't need to be told twice. His eyes never left Elizabeth's face as they nodded and smiled their way through the other guests.

"Elizabeth, Miss Holloway, good evening," said Avery.

Gideon's attention was drawn briefly to Miss Holloway, whose cheeks were delicately flushed. She spared only a quick glance in his direction before returning her gaze to the viscount.

"Good evening, Avery. Captain Sparks," said Elizabeth, shooting him a strangely hostile glance.

"Lady Elizabeth, Miss Holloway," he replied politely.

"No need to go any further," said Avery. "It's a sad crush."

"Mrs. Sinclair must be pleased," said Penelope.

Elizabeth shook her head and said, "We have to go on, Avery. I want everyone to see that Penelope is in town."

"Yes, it is a good way to meet a great deal of people in a very small length of time and in a very small space," said the viscount. "Then we will not keep you. Where do you go from here?"

"We are going home to fetch Mimi, and then we will go to Lady Hazelton's musicale."

"Perhaps we will see you there," said the viscount.

Then the two ladies were swept away by the crowd, leaving Gideon and Avery to struggle toward the door and freedom.

"Hazelton. Isn't that the name of the popinjay who told us about Wakefield's little society?" asked Gideon when they were outside.

"One and the same. Lady Hazelton is his doting mother. She fancies herself a singer, so she loves giving these little musicales."

"And we are going to it tonight?"

"We weren't until Elizabeth said that she would be there. Opportunities, old boy. We have to take advantage of every opportunity. Besides, Lady Hazelton always sets a superb buffet supper for her victims . . . uh, I mean, guests, of course."

Chapter Seven

Lady Hazelton's musicale was well under way when Elizabeth, Penelope, and Lady Louisa arrived. Their hostess, a large lady with a bulbous nose, greeted them and whispered that they should find a seat and make themselves comfortable.

When Elizabeth and her party arrived, she spotted the captain and steered her friend to another location. Despite Roger's casual attitude toward the captain, Penelope might still find it difficult being in close company with the man who was behind her brother's misfortune.

"There are three seats together," said Lady Louisa. "Oh, and look, Avery is there with his friend, Captain Sparks." Elizabeth shot her grandmother a speaking look, and Lady Louisa added, "But we would have to make our way past too many chairs. Let us sit down back here."

When they were seated, Penny leaned close to Elizabeth and said, "Really, Elizabeth, I do not mind meeting Captain Sparks. I cannot hold a grudge when Roger has forgiven him."

"I commend you for your goodness, Penny, but I prefer sitting back here anyway. We can slip out for some refreshments and miss some of the program." Elizabeth looked away and applauded dutifully as the young lady singing finished her piece on the pianoforte.

"Oh no," whispered Lady Louisa. "I thought we had arrived late enough that we would miss Lady Hazelton's performance. Oh dear, my head is already aching."

Elizabeth giggled, and Penelope asked, "What is the matter with Lady Hazelton's voi . . . oh, dear." She covered her mouth to contain her laughter while Lady Hazelton headed for a high note in her aria—not that she actually made it, but she gave it a valiant and vociferous effort.

"Sh! Do not start giggling, or I will disgrace myself," said Lady Louisa, raising her fan to cover her face.

It was a long, arduous aria. Guests were wiggling in their seats as if trying to escape the piercing notes.

"She made that one," said a deep voice behind them.

Recognizing her brother's voice, Elizabeth turned and admonished, "Val, do keep your voice down."

"Why tell me? You ought to be telling Lady Hazelton. Everyone ought to be telling Lady Hazelton. Come with me, Elizabeth. I need to talk to you."

"Again?" she said.

Val slipped away, and Elizabeth followed as discreetly as she could. She followed him down a long corridor and into what appeared to be a library.

Shutting the door, Val sagged against it and said, "Egad! What an atrocious sound!"

"Thank you for saving me from it, but how did you know where you were going?"

"Lady Hazelton and I are old friends. Well, her daughter and I are."

"Good heavens, Val. Emily is a married lady!"

"And all alone until her husband's recent return from the wars." Those blue eyes twinkled, and she had to smile. "Besides, it was short-lived, and we parted ways quite pleased with one another."

"Never mind all that. What did you want to see me about? You received the bank draft, did you not?"

"Yes, and why do you think I needed to talk to you about money? No, no, do not say why. I wanted to see if I could have the use of a hack from your stable."

"You know that you can. Just see Mr. Cochran."

"Well, the thing is, I am not in his good books just now. Not since last fall when I . . ."

"Tried to gamble away my carriage team."

"Only one of them," he said with a laugh.

"One of a matched pair. Not only was it dishonest, it was also stupid. You should never separate a matched pair."

"I know, I know. But will you write him a note telling him it is all right?" asked Val.

"Yes, I will send it to him first thing tomorrow."

Her brother kissed her cheek and then said, "Early tomorrow? It is just that I have plans to attend a little picnic."

"Do you mean the Donovans' alfresco breakfast? That is not until next week."

"No, not that. Something of a more private nature."

"Oh, Val! You are going to land in the suds again! Who is it this time?" asked Elizabeth.

"Do you really wish to know?"

Elizabeth sighed and said, "No, I suppose not. Only do try to keep your name out of the scandal sheets this Season."

"That is forever an objective of mine, dear sister. Now, I will let you return to your torture." He opened the door and listened as the music finally came to an end. "Just in time. She will be announcing that the buffet is ready now. Emily told me her mother was upset that people always left early, after the supper was served. So she decided to sing first and then have supper."

"Well, we may accuse her of being tone deaf, but not of stupidity," said Elizabeth. She rapped his arm with her fan and said, "Just listen to me! You are a bad influence on me, Val."

"If I must be an influence on anyone, let it be a bad one. Anything else would damage my reputation. Good night, love."

"Good night."

Elizabeth hurried back to the other guests, who were moving toward the dining room. Penny and her grandmother were nowhere to be seen, but Avery waved to her, and she joined him.

"This had better be worth it," he whispered in her ear.

"You sound like Val."

He looked wounded, and she said, "Not exactly like him. For one thing, he would not have whispered it."

"I saw him come in. Where has he gone?"

"I did not ask. It is better not knowing. Oh, hello again, Captain Sparks."

"Hello. Might we have the pleasure of your company for supper?"

"I must find my grandmother and Penny."

"I will help you," he said, looking over the tops of the heads of most of the people. "There she is. Why don't I escort you over there and then fetch you a plate?"

"That is hardly necessary, Captain. I will have no trouble reaching them. The crowd is not that large. Besides, you should probably not eat with us. It might upset Penelope."

"Why the dev . . . why should my presence upset your friend?"

"Do you remember when we met in the park, and Penny turned so white?" He nodded, and Elizabeth continued, "It was learning your identity that upset her. Her brother is Roger Holloway, the man who lost his leg in a battle at sea when your ship fired on his."

"By Jove!" said Avery.

Gideon shook his head and said, "Then of course I should not join you for dinner. I should simply leave."

"No, no," said Elizabeth, laying her hand on his sleeve. "I am sorry to have been so blunt, especially when Penelope has forgiven you."

"Why? I should think she would hate me."

She clutched at his sleeve and said, "Not at all. Oh, she was upset upon hearing your name, but after she spoke to her brother, she realized she was just being foolish. Roger holds no grudges, and neither does she."

"Come on, Captain, you might as well face her."

"Are you sure?" he asked, looking into Elizabeth's concerned gaze.

She gave him a little smile and nodded.

Gideon said, "Then I will apologize immediately."

"Why don't you call on Roger tomorrow instead?"

"I could do that," said Gideon.

"Good, that's all settled. I'm going to get something to eat. Anyone care to join me?"

Elizabeth released her hold on Gideon's sleeve. "I believe you were going to fix my plate, Captain?"

"Yes, my lady. I will bring it to you in a trice."

She giggled and protested, "But you have no idea what I might like."

"Want to place a wager on that?" muttered her cousin. He smiled when she frowned at him.

"Why don't you let me surprise you? I think I have a pretty good idea of what a lady might like."

She rolled her eyes and said, "Oh, do you? You have such boundless experience with ladies that you can simply divine which dishes might appeal to us? I should warn you, Captain, that I am not like other ladies."

With a flash of teeth, he said, "Is that a wager, my lady?"

Elizabeth lifted her chin and said, "Done!"

"For what stakes?" he asked, his voice soft and velvety, just the way it had been in her dreams.

Those dratted dreams! "Any stakes you like, sir."

"If I win, you will owe me a . . . kiss."

"Predictable," she said. "And when I win?"

"What shall it be? You name it."

Her green eyes sparkled with mischief, and she said, "You will take part in tonight's musicale by volunteering to sing."

"I cannot sing, but I will play the pianoforte."

Elizabeth sniffed and said, "Very well, then it is settled. I will see you shortly. Remember, I must find nothing on the plate objectionable, or you lose."

Elizabeth hurried away, confident that she had already won their wager.

He will make one fatal mistake, she thought with a grin. *He will include a strawberry or two. Everyone likes strawberries.* She grinned. *Everyone except me!*

By the time she joined Lady Louisa and Penny, they were already eating.

"What happened to you? I thought you had abandoned us," said Lady Louisa.

"Not at all. I just got behind the crowd."

"But where is your plate?"

"Oh, it is coming. Captain Sparks asked if he might fill my plate."

"How gallant of him," said Lady Louisa. "Such a gentleman."

"Oh, he is the most perfect of gentlemen. However, we have a wager on whether he can fill my plate just as I wish. His forfeit will be volunteering to play the pianoforte for everyone."

Her grandmother's eyes danced, and she asked, "And your forfeit, should he succeed?"

"Nothing."

"Nothing? That is a very odd sort of bet," said her grandmother.

Elizabeth blushed and mumbled, "A kiss. That would be my forfeit if I lose, but I cannot do so."

Penelope giggled and said, "Either way, I think you win, Liz. He is very handsome."

"Really? I hardly noticed."

They watched Avery and the captain walking toward them. The captain set the plate he carried on the table.

Two big, ripe strawberries stared back at Elizabeth, and she said, "Aha! You have already lost! I cannot abide strawberries!"

"And how is that? You have not even seen your plate yet. That is my plate. This one is yours, my lady." With a flourish, he produced another plate from behind his back and set it before her with an elegant bow.

"You told him, Avery! That is unfair."

"I never said a word! Cross my heart!"

"Is everything to your liking, my lady?" asked Gideon.

"No! That is, yes. Everything is fine." He watched her for a moment, and she snapped, "Well surely you do not wish to receive your kiss now!"

"Oh, I see. Yes, quite right. Not at all the proper thing for a gentleman to do in public. Very well then. I will be patient."

Lady Louisa rolled her eyes, and Elizabeth frowned at her. "Thank you, Captain."

She pushed the plate away, and the captain said, "Are you not going to eat?"

"I have lost my appetite," she replied.

"Elizabeth! You are being a bad sport!" said her cousin.

"Nevertheless, I could not eat a bite now."

To his credit, if the captain was annoyed, he didn't show it. Instead, he smiled and excused himself for a moment. Elizabeth watched him cross the large room and speak to Lady Hazelton. Oh, those shoulders.

When he returned and sat down, he began eating without saying a word.

Elizabeth's curiosity got the best of her, and she asked, "What was that about, Captain Sparks?"

"I was just arranging with Lady Hazelton to play for everyone after supper."

"But you did not lose the wager," she said.

"But I did. The plate is not pleasing to you. I believe that is how we stated the wager. Therefore, I have lost and will gladly settle my wager in the honorable manner."

"But the kiss!" said Lady Louisa. With a little gasp, she covered her mouth. "So sorry."

Elizabeth plucked up her courage and asked softly, "What about that kiss?"

"The kiss is yours to give away where you will. I did not earn it," said Gideon.

"Only because I was behaving badly," she said.

His smile was full of understanding, and he replied softly, "I cannot believe you would ever behave badly, Lady Elizabeth."

"You are too kind," she whispered.

"Much too kind," muttered her cousin.

"Avery!" said Elizabeth.

Their audience was losing interest, and Avery said, "Fine. You shall kiss him, and he shall play for us. Only one thing, Gideon. Your playing had better be easier on the ears than Lady Hazelton's . . . oh, hello, Lady Hazelton. Another superb evening of entertainment."

"You are too kind, Lord Winters. Captain, I thought you might like to try out the instrument while most of the guests are still eating. Just to get a feel for the keys."

"Thank you, my lady. I will do just that as soon as I have finished this excellent meal."

"Well, you know where it is when you are ready."

Elizabeth pushed her food back and forth on her plate, taking a bite now and then while the conversation floated around her. The captain was very different from the prude she had met at the inn. He was also not the arrogant man from the stables. There was more to this one than met the eye.

She glanced up to find him watching her. He smiled, and she ducked her head, again pretending an intense interest in her food.

The captain excused himself a moment later. She watched him as he walked away, stopping at a table for two and chatting for a moment with its occupants. He appeared to be the perfect English gentleman—despite being an American. There was something more to him, but Elizabeth was not sure what it was. She wasn't even sure she liked it, or him.

In disgust she pushed her plate away.

There was still the question of that kiss. She felt sure he would not forget about it.

And Elizabeth knew it was foremost on her mind!

"Are you coming, Liz?" asked Penny.

"Yes, yes, of course." She dabbed at her mouth and looked around to see that most of the guests were strolling back to the ballroom. She could already hear the tinkling sounds of the pianoforte.

It was a haunting melody. Something new. At least, she had never heard it before.

When she was seated again, she was spellbound—not only by the music, but by the far away gleam in the Captain's eyes as he played. His technique was flawless, but it was the passion that appealed to her.

His eyes found hers. He pursed his lips ever so slightly and then winked at her.

Elizabeth found herself blushing like a just-kissed schoolgirl. She smiled and dropped her eyes.

When she looked up again, he was still watching her, his dark eyes dancing with amusement.

She lifted her nose and looked away.

She would not let an upstart American turn her world upside down. And he thought she owed him a kiss! Never in a million years would she submit to such a . . . disgraceful . . .

The music rose in a crescendo to the passionate, crashing finale.

Kiss.

The next afternoon, Elizabeth was watching out the window when her cousin and the captain arrived to pay a call. She twitched the curtain back into place and hurried to the sofa. She heard Roberts answer the door, and there followed a rumble of low, masculine voices. Picking up her needlework, she waited for the door to open . . . and waited . . . and waited.

Finally, in a fit of pique, Elizabeth got on her feet and strolled toward the door of the drawing room. Her actions a study in casualness, she opened it and stepped into the empty hall.

Roberts appeared from the back of the house, and she said, "I thought I heard men's voices."

"Yes, my lady. It was Lord Winters and a Captain Sparks."

"Well? Where are they?"

"Oh, they came to see Mr. Holloway. I have just taken them back to his study."

She just stood there, and after a moment, the butler asked, "Will there be anything else, my lady?"

"No, nothing," she said, turning on her heel and retreating to the drawing room. She picked up her needlework again, proceeded to prick her finger, and pitched it on the table. That was it! She would not sit idly by, waiting on them to come and speak to her. She would simply go out to the shops.

Elizabeth relentlessly silenced the small voice that told her she was being childish. She returned to the hall and paused there, listening. Roberts looked at her, and she said, "Please order my horse to be brought round as soon as possible."

"Very good, my lady."

Walking to the stairs, Elizabeth heard raucous male laughter coming from the small library where Roger was working on his book. She stifled her impatience and reminded herself that she wanted Roger to enjoy his time in London, too. If conversing with the man who had caused his mishap made Roger happy, then she would not quibble about it.

She could not pretend to understand why, either. Men! They were such difficult creatures!

* * *

"Dash it all, man! She's at it again!" grumbled the viscount as he entered Gideon's sitting room.

"She?"

"My grandmother. I have a note from her that says she wants to be certain we are early tonight."

"A summons from the queen, eh? I suppose she wants me there early so she can inspect my fingernails," said Gideon.

He glanced at his image in the glass and gave a grunt of approval. He would do. The black silk coat and snowy cravat would make anyone look a proper gentleman. The countess could not quibble at his appearance if she were in a quibbling sort of mood—which she usually was.

"I suppose she means well," said the viscount.

"I know, but I can't help but feel that her advice about Elizabeth has been inaccurate, to say the least. Only look how your cousin treated me after the incident at the inn. I tried to act the perfect gentleman and instead acted the perfect fool. But at the musicale, when I demanded a kiss as a forfeit, Elizabeth was quick to respond."

As they headed out the door to stroll to Grosvenor Square, Avery said, "That's what happens when you listen to an old woman—especially one as prim and proper as my grandmother." With a smug smile, he added, "Like I said, I should have had more of a hand in your training where it comes to the ladies."

"So you think I overdid the gentlemanly conduct?" asked Gideon.

"No, not exactly, but only look at it from Elizabeth's point of view. From the story you told me about the inn, you practically threw her out of the private parlor, as if you could not bear to be in the same room with her."

"But I explained that! I told her that the last thing I wanted was for us to have to get married because I had compromised her . . . hellfire and damnation!" exclaimed Gideon. "What a perfect prig I was! No wonder she . . . I am lucky that she even speaks to me!" He punctuated this with a string of oaths while Avery clutched his sides, laughing uproariously.

"And you! Of all times for you to be sick!" said Gideon.

Avery caught his breath and said, "Oh, I wish I had been well enough to have been downstairs and listened in at the door. My God, man! You may as well have told her she had horns and a snout!"

Again those terrible oaths, but this time, Gideon ended with, "I must apologize at once!"

"Now, steady, old boy. In my experience, it doesn't do to revisit such a delicate situation. You will only reopen the wound. Best to let sleeping dogs lie."

"Perhaps you are right. Still, I wish there were some way to make amends for such a terrible gaffe."

"Well, you could always collect on that wager. That should do the trick."

Gideon slapped his forhead and stopped in his tracks. Avery took his arm and dragged him along.

"The kiss. Devil take me! I even turned down a kiss with her. I was just trying to be a gentle . . . I will tell you one thing, Winters, I am done trying to be the perfect gentleman. Every time, I put my foot in it."

"You do seem to have bad luck at it. Still, perhaps she really does like that sort of thing. I mean, having her suitors moon over her like sick calves hasn't worked. Perhaps your rejections will only serve to intrigue her, to pique her interest, as it were."

"You are full of rot, aren't you," said Gideon with a laugh. "Still, it has taught me one thing. Your cousin is a patient woman. She should have slapped my face the first time we met and been done with it. Perhaps I do still stand a chance. Tonight, I will . . ."

"Not tonight. Not in front of Grandmother."

"Frankly, Winters, I could not care less what your grandmother thinks of my tactics. Hers certainly haven't worked. When I have the chance, I shall tell Elizabeth how beautiful she is, and how much I admire her."

"If you insist," came the viscount's doubtful comment.

"I do," said Gideon.

"Well, then, here we are. I look forward to witnessing the battle."

"If it were a battle, I would know what sort of strategies would work, and come what may, I would not question my position. I am more than thirty years old, not a lad. If I had followed my own instincts, I would have shared that parlor with her, gotten to know her, and, if my luck held, received that kiss all in the same night."

Just then, Finch opened the door and welcomed them inside. They went straight to the drawing room, which was filled with the Rotherfords' closest friends. Gideon spotted Elizabeth immediately. She was wearing a silk gown of emerald green, the color of her eyes. Around her neck was a simple string of pearls; another strand coiled around her hair. She was the most beautiful woman in the room.

After speaking to the earl and the countess, Gideon exchanged a few words with Lady Louisa. Then he headed straight for the sofa where Elizabeth sat with her brother, Val. Roger Holloway's chair faced them and his sister, Penelope, perched on a delicate chair beside him. Gideon took the empty seat on the sofa between Elizabeth and her brother.

"Good evening," he said in general.

"Good evening, Captain," came the chorus of replies.

"You ladies are looking lovely tonight."

While Elizabeth looked down and mumbled a reply, Penelope said, "Thank you, Captain. I am so glad that you visited Roger this afternoon and persuaded him to come tonight."

"Penny," said her brother.

"You did that?" murmured Elizabeth, lifting her face so that he could look into those lovely eyes.

"Of course. It was selfish on my part, of course. Nothing like having another seaman to talk to."

He grinned at Roger, who nodded in agreement and said, "Yes, you ladies will probably be sorry before the evening is over because you will feel so neglected."

"There are other gentlemen present," said Penny with a surreptitious glance across the room at the viscount. She lowered her gaze when he noticed her and came to join them.

Gazing at Penny, Avery said, "You are looking jolly pretty, uh, both of you."

"Very glib," muttered Gideon.

"I beg your pardon, Captain?" said Elizabeth, once again looking up at him. This time, there was mischief gleaming in her eyes.

"Oh, nothing," he replied, smiling down at her.

Her attention was diverted as her grandfather waved at her. Rising, she said, "Excuse me. There is an old friend of the family I should speak to."

Gideon watched her join her grandfather, who was talking to another man of perhaps forty years, with thick gray hair. Gideon felt a twinge of jealousy.

Avery took the seat Elizabeth had vacated and nudged him with his elbow. "Old friend of the family."

"Who, my lord?" asked Penelope.

"The fellow Elizabeth and Grandfather are talking to. You may remember him from your visits to Wintersford. He owns the property to the east. Witherspoon is his name."

"That is Mr. Witherspoon?" said Penelope, her eyes growing wide. Then she giggled. The three gentlemen looked at her expectantly. "Oh, I see I shall have to explain. When we were mere schoolgirls, Elizabeth and I fancied ourselves in love with Mr. Witherspoon. In truth, I was the one who was in love with him. Elizabeth always had an eye out for that friend of yours, Landon Wakefield."

"It is Sir Landon Wakefield now," said Avery.

"Oh, good for him," she said.

Avery asked, "And what do you think of your Mr. Witherspoon now, Miss Holloway?"

"Well, he is as handsome as ever. More mature looking, with his hair almost entirely gray, but still quite a striking figure." She rose and the three gentlemen did the same. "If you will excuse me, I think I will just go over and have a word."

"Just who is this Witherspoon?" said the captain.

"Angus Witherspoon is accounted quite a scholar," said Roger. "I have read his translations on the great battle of Salamis, and I quite agreed with the conclusions he came to about their trireme ships. I should very much like to speak to him."

Gideon said quickly, "Then let me wheel you over there, Holloway. I would be interested in what he has to say, too."

The viscount snickered at this and moved away to speak to other guests. Val took himself off to another group of guests, mostly females.

As Gideon pushed the Bath chair, he asked, "What did Witherspoon have to say about the . . . trireme, you said?"

"He compared it to the privateers you Americans used against us in the late war, like the one you were commanding when we, uh, met."

"Really?" What else could Gideon say? And here he was using this man to keep an eye on Elizabeth. She was watching his approach and, by the look on her face, she was not impressed by him in the least. He wondered what he had done—or not done—now.

Penelope said, "Mr. Witherspoon, allow me to introduce my brother, Roger Holloway. And this is Captain Sparks."

"How do you do?" said the older man. "Holloway. Yes,

now I remember. I read an article you wrote about privateers."

"I am gratified that you remember it, sir," said Roger.

"I remember very well because you quoted something I had said in my book."

"Yes, I did. I thought your comparison of the Greeks in the battle of Salamis in 480 BC to the American privateers fascinating. Captain Sparks, by the way, commanded one of those ships, commissioned by the United States government, of course."

"Did you, sir? Perhaps the three of us could have a few words after supper."

"It would be a pleasure," said Gideon.

Laying her gloved hand on Witherspoon's coat sleeve and smiling up at him, Elizabeth said, "I hope it will be when you gentlemen are enjoying your port."

He patted that hand and said, "Certainly, my dear. We would not dream of boring you ladies with our old stories."

Elizabeth simpered, and Gideon wanted to wring her neck. What game was she playing? Or was it a game at all? Had she not married because she enjoyed playing the flirt too much? He was tempted to ask her just that.

Fortunately for Gideon, Finch entered and announced that supper was served.

Chapter Eight

There were some thirty guests for supper that evening. The dining room was ablaze with candles, but the fireplaces on either side of the table were dark. Still, with all the people it contained, the room was warm enough and quite comfortable.

Gideon found the countess had seated him next to Elizabeth. Here was his chance to make amends for his insults. Not that he had intended to insult her by saying that he didn't wish to compromise her, didn't wish to marry her, and then later, that he managed to lose that wager so that he wouldn't even have to kiss her. In truth, kissing her and marrying her were foremost in his mind.

Once seated, Gideon found himself staring at those sweet lips as these thoughts raced through his mind. Unfortunately, he had not been attending to her conversation and had no idea how to reply.

"I, uh, excuse me. I didn't quite hear . . ." he stammered.

"I asked if you were enjoying London," said Elizabeth.

"Yes, yes. It is quite pleasant. So many interesting people."

She smiled politely and asked, "Being so far away from home, do you not miss your friends and family?"

"I have few friends and no family, my lady. I was raised by my grandfather, and he has been dead for a dozen or more years."

"How sad for you, Captain. But surely there are friends who miss you."

"Certainly there are some. I don't wish to say I am friendless, but I have made many new friends since I arrived. Your cousin, for one, has been most kind. As indeed, has your entire family."

"I fear that my family can be a little overbearing at times," she said, stirring her soup.

"But your grandmother, Lady Louisa, is wonderful."

"Mimi is a dear. Grandmother is also a wonderful lady, but she tries so hard to be a tyrant. I fear she sometimes succeeds," she added with a small laugh.

Entranced by the sound, he murmured, "And she cheats at cards."

"Grandmother?" she exclaimed. When several heads turned, she lowered her voice and said, "Who told you that?"

"I experienced it firsthand, but Lady Louisa warned me about it."

"Oh, dear," she whispered. "I do hope you were not playing for high stakes."

"Not at all. As a matter of fact, the neighbors began to arrive, and we never played the hand. Of course, it was not for money, only for points and the glory of winning."

"That is good to know, but what a lowering thought. I knew she liked to win, but I never dreamed she would go so far."

Elizabeth giggled and smiled up at him. Gideon thought his heart would melt. All strategies flew from his mind. All he wanted was to pull her into his embrace and kiss her senseless.

Instead, he winked at her and said, "Sh. This is to go no further. It will be our secret."

"Our secret," she said with a nod. With this, she turned and began conversing with the gentleman on her left.

This freed Gideon to converse with Lady Winters, who

was on his right. This lady, however, seemed intent on conversing solely with the gentleman on her other side. No doubt the countess had instructed her daughter-in-law not to monopolize him during dinner.

Turning back to Elizabeth, he found she was still occupied with her other dinner partner. He sat in silence for several minutes. Finally, Gideon started talking to himself.

"Hasn't the weather been beautiful this spring? Why, yes, it has been exceptionally fine. Did you chance to go to the theater the other night and watch the performance of *Othello?* Yes, I did. I believe I saw you there. Weren't you sitting in Lord Winters' box?"

"What are you doing?" hissed Elizabeth.

"Oh, pardon me. I believe Lady Elizabeth has addressed me. Very kind of her, don't you think?"

"I said, what are you doing?"

"I am having an unexceptional dinner conversation. Quiet, dignified, and completely devoid of anything controversial or interesting."

"Yes, I heard that. But with whom were you speaking?" she asked.

"Myself. I often converse with myself when there is no one else present to talk to. Sometimes it is the only intelligent conversation available."

Elizabeth smiled and said, "But, Captain, you are in the middle of a room filled with interesting people."

"So I am," he replied, looking around and feigning surprise. Then he shrugged and said, "However, with you busy talking to that crusty looking gentleman on your other side and Lady Winters busy conversing with the man on her right, I am quite without a dinner partner. Therefore, I am talking to myself. Or rather, I was until you interrupted."

"Interrupted?" said Elizabeth, her tone frosty. "Then perhaps I should allow you to return to your solo conversation."

"No, I'm afraid I cannot. He is put out with me for speaking to you for too long and refuses to open his mouth again," said Gideon.

"You are absurd," she said with a giggle.

He gazed at her intently and said, "Only desperate for your company, my lady."

She dropped her eyes, and Gideon knew that he had overstepped whatever invisible boundary she placed around her.

Before Elizabeth could turn away again, he said lightly, "What man would not be desperate for the pleasure of your company?"

He glanced around the table, took a bite of his soup, and swallowed before saying quite casually, "Lady Louisa is looking very well tonight. I am glad to see that she doesn't pine for her garden when she is in town."

Elizabeth appeared relieved to have the conversation return to mundane topics, and she said, "Not at all. She enjoys the social Season, and besides, she has a small but lovely garden to play in at my house."

"Oh, yes, your cousin told me that it was your house we visited earlier, when we went to see Roger Holloway."

She nodded and said, "I bought it almost two years ago. My other grandmother, as you know, can be a little difficult to live with. So when I am in the country, I am happy to stay at Wintersford, where we are not constantly bumping shoulders. But in town, I have my own house. It also gives Mimi, Lady Louisa, a place of refuge now that her nephew and his wife take up residence in the Upton town house."

"How do you keep it all straight?" asked Gideon.

"Keep what straight?"

"All the family. Not having a family, it seems very confusing to me."

Elizabeth laughed quietly and said, "In the *ton*, almost everyone is related to everyone else in some manner. Keeping track of all the bloodlines is just part of the job."

"I suppose so. Now, what about your brother? He is not related to Lord Rotherford?"

"No, Valentine's father is Baron Lightfoot, although he prefers to be addressed as Mr. Lightfoot. He lives in the country the year round."

"And your mother?" he asked.

Elizabeth gave a shrug of her slender shoulders and said, "She remains in the country, too. I had hoped to persuade her to come to town—to see Val, if nothing else—but she was . . . unable to get away."

He could hear the bitterness in her words. She looked up suddenly and blushed. "I am sorry. I am talking too much, and about people you don't even know. Not the trait of a good conversationalist. Tell me, Captain, have you been all over the world?"

"Our side of the world. I have not sailed in the Pacific Ocean. Someday, perhaps. They say the water is as blue as the Mediterranean, and I would like to see that. Have you traveled much?"

A faraway look in her eyes, she said, "No, but I do hope to see Paris soon, now that everything has quieted down."

"I went once, on business. It is very pretty, but I prefer England. The language barrier, you know."

"*Vous ne parlez pas français?*"

"*Mais oui, mademoiselle!* I do speak French, but as you can tell my accent is atrocious and they are always correcting me, trying to improve it. You English hear me, know I am an American, and accept the fact that I am nothing but a provincial—unworthy or incapable of change."

"Now you are exaggerating, Captain. I cannot believe that anyone thinks that about you. Why, one has only to look at you to know that you frequent the best tailors, attend the best dinner parties, and know only the best people."

"Like you," said Gideon, raising his glass to her. When

they had taken wine together, he added, "By outward appearance, I am as much a cultured gentleman as your cousin, Lord Winters. However, unlike what Poor Richard says, clothes do not necessarily make the man, my lady."

"But you must admit, they do help," she said with a laugh.

He smiled and acquiesced. Elizabeth turned to speak to the man on her other side, and Gideon was left wondering if he had furthered his cause or hindered it.

He was pleased that she had found his nonsensical conversation with himself amusing. But had she enjoyed the rest of their conversation? It was impossible to say.

For the duration of the meal, when she blessed him with her attention, their conversation was quite conventional. Not boring, Gideon told himself. It could never be boring to watch her eyes dance, her lips move, or hear the sound of her voice.

Oh, I have it bad, thought Gideon. *So bad, it is almost frightening.*

He was beginning to wonder how he would manage if he did not win her. Before, his life had held little promise. He had been penniless and without a ship. Now, he didn't want to think how he would feel if he failed to win her heart.

On this black note, Gideon was almost relieved when the countess rose and signaled the ladies that it was time to leave the gentlemen to the cigars and port.

Cards and conversation were the order of the evening. Lady Rotherford soon had more than half of them—mostly the older guests—seated at tables with cards before them. Gideon was amused to see that Lady Rotherford did not suggest he play cards. He supposed it was because Elizabeth was not playing.

Gideon sat beside Roger's chair, talking about ships

and the sea. While the young people chatted, the ladies took turns displaying their talent on the pianoforte.

The quiet Miss Fanshaw, up from the country for her Season, played a complicated piece that resulted in a flurry of applause when she was finished. Remembering the dinner at Wintersford, Gideon went to speak to her. The countess glared at him, and he smiled and nodded to her in return.

"Are you enjoying London, Miss Fanshaw?" he asked.

"Yes, Captain, though I miss home."

"I hope your friend's journey to his uncle's home yielded the result he desired."

When she smiled, her face became luminous. He leaned forward to catch her quiet remarks. "Yes, we . . . he was very pleased."

"Then should I be offering my congratulations?" asked Gideon.

"No, not yet. My mother still insists that I have my Season before we announce the betrothal."

"A wise woman, but since you have made me privy to your plans, I will wish you congratulations in advance."

Gideon lifted her hand to his lips and kissed it. Miss Fanshaw's mother called her daughter to her side.

He returned to his seat and was surprised—and pleased—when Elizabeth joined them.

"I did not realize you were acquainted with Miss Fanshaw, Captain."

"We met at Wintersford. She is a very sensible young lady. I enjoyed talking to her that night."

"Yes, she was always a sweet child," said Elizabeth.

Just then, someone called on Elizabeth to take her turn at the pianoforte. She declined immediately, and her brother seconded that, saying baldly, as brothers are wont to do, that his sister had absolutely no musical talent.

Elizabeth's gaze fell on Gideon. With a smile, she said, "I know someone who could take my place. Won't you play for us, Captain?"

"If you like," he replied. He might prefer sitting quietly beside her and exploring her seeming jealousy of Miss Fanshaw, but he could deny her nothing.

Going to the pianoforte, Gideon sat down and took a deep breath before beginning another haunting tune. All conversation stopped. Even the card players fell silent as he poured his heart into the music.

When it was over, the applause was genuine. Gideon bowed and gave up the instrument to yet another young lady.

As Gideon returned to the seat beside Elizabeth, she said, "That was as beautiful as last night's performance, and another piece I am not familiar with. What is it called?"

"I haven't named it," he replied quietly.

"You wrote it?" asked Roger. "Never knew anyone so talented, Captain."

Elizabeth asked, "And the one last night? Did you write that one, too?"

"Yes. I had a pianoforte on board my ship. When you have an excellent crew and a calm sea, there is time for all sorts of hobbies," he explained.

"But why don't you name your compositions? You ought to do so and have them published," said Elizabeth.

"I have never considered that a possibility. I write music for myself."

"Then at least give them a name," she said.

"Very well," said Gideon, smiling down at her, his dark gaze warm and compelling. "I shall call this evening's song, 'Elizabeth's Sonnet,' and last night's will be 'Elizabeth's Serenade.'"

Her eyes turned cold, and she said, "Be serious, sir."

Still smiling, he said, "I am serious. You say the compositions are beautiful. You are beautiful, too, so I will name them after you. Doesn't that please you?"

Judging from the scowl on her face, he knew he had made a faux pas. What was it Lord Winters had warned him about? Her other suitors had gone overboard on the flowery compliments, and they had failed.

She pursed her lips and snapped, "You need not make game of me."

Trying to recover, he allowed his temper free rein. "Make game of you? I am trying to pay you a compliment, woman," growled Gideon.

Rising, she snapped, "A strange sort of compliment!"

Gideon scrambled to his feet, but Elizabeth had already stormed away. He took one step to pursue her, but thought better of it. Sitting down again, he was glad to see Roger Holloway's look of empathy.

"Women!"

"Yes," said Roger with a glimmer of a smile. "Completely inexplicable creatures."

Just then, Valentine Lightfoot clapped his hands to gain everyone's attention.

"Who would like to liven things up a bit? Let's play musical chairs!"

His suggestion was greeted with enthusiasm by the younger guests, and servants were called to bring chairs and arrange them by pairs, back to back, in a long row.

One of the young ladies volunteered to play the pianoforte. His jaw still clenched in irritation, Gideon declined their invitation to play.

Roger Holloway tapped Gideon on the arm and said, "Try to understand Elizabeth's point of view, Captain."

Gideon sat down beside him again, but he was still too aggravated to reply.

Roger said sensibly, "Elizabeth has been courted and complimented every Season for the past six or eight years. Can you blame her for not believing in your compliments?"

"What others have said in the past has nothing to do with what I say to her. Am I to be insulted because of past suitors?" came Gideon's stubborn reply.

"I am sure you meant it as a compliment, Captain, but

she has had too many poems written to her hair, her eyes, and so forth to put any faith in such flowery sentiments. She and Penelope used to sit and read them out loud to each other."

"Lady Elizabeth is a cynic," said Gideon.

Roger shook his head and murmured, "That is a harsh description for such a kind lady."

Miss Stout began to play, and the column of young people started marching around the chairs. Suddenly the music stopped and everyone scrambled. In the end, one gentleman was left standing. To calls of friendly mockery, he took a seat on the nearest sofa, and the play continued with one less chair.

"Look at her," said Roger Holloway.

Gideon obediently looked at Elizabeth, whose cheeks were infused with a delicate pink. "She is beautiful."

Shaking his head, Roger said, "Not Elizabeth. I meant my sister. I haven't seen Penelope look that lively in four years. Longer than that, actually, since I was gone for a year before . . ." He looked at Gideon and coughed. "Sorry, I didn't mean to bring that up. It always makes everyone else more uncomfortable than it does me."

"Think nothing of it, and your sister does not appear sad in the least," said Gideon. "She always has a smile on her face. As a matter of fact, she seems happiest when she is with you."

"Perhaps, and I don't mean to say that she is sad. Penny is too kind to be sad about having to look after me. And, to be honest, we rub along very well together. It's just good to see her enjoying herself."

They laughed as another person had to sit out and another chair was removed. Lord Winters was next, and after him, a giggling Penelope joined them when she was left standing.

"You should have played, Captain!" she said, her eyes still shining.

"Another time, Miss Holloway."

Soon, the game had dwindled to Elizabeth and Mr. Gilbert. As the lively music began again, they walked quickly round and round. The music stopped, and they scrambled for the remaining chair while the others laughed and shouted encouragement.

Though each one used his weight to gain the seat, Elizabeth lost her balance and landed on the floor with a resounding thump. She was laughing so hard that she could hardly catch her breath. Her face was red with the exertion, and Gideon thought she had never looked more beautiful.

He hurried forward to help her to her feet.

"Thank you, Captain," she said, smiling at him in a way that let him know their little misunderstanding was forgotten.

With a curtsy to the winner, Elizabeth said, "I demand a rematch, Mr. Gilbert."

"Another night, perhaps. I may have ended the winner, Lady Elizabeth, but it is a hollow victory to win over a beautiful lady such as you are." Mr. Gilbert swept her an elegant bow and kissed her hand. Looking up, he said, "Ah, and here is the tea tray."

Without a backward glance, the young man hurried over to the table where the footmen had placed the huge silver trays.

"So much for his compliment," muttered Gideon. "Now I see why you scoffed at mine. They don't mean much in Society."

Elizabeth chuckled and said, "Sometimes they are genuine, but you do understand why I was not swept away by your comment. On the other hand, I should have been more gracious. I hope you will forgive me."

"Without hesitation, my lady. I was wondering if I might take you for a drive in the park tomorrow afternoon."

"I am already engaged to drive with someone else. Perhaps another day?"

They rejoined Roger Holloway. Avery, seated next

to Penelope, moved over to allow Elizabeth to sit down, but she was summoned by her grandmother to help pour out.

Watching her walk away, Gideon kicked himself for not exacting a day and time for their drive. Any chance for inimate conversation was past, however, and for Gideon, the evening was over.

Elizabeth climbed out of bed and stretched. Her maid entered with a tray of steaming chocolate, and she padded over to the tray and accepted the cup.

"Another beautiful day, Dulcie."

"Yes, my lady," said the maid. Shaking her head in disapproval as always, Dulcie asked, "Do you wish me to have your horse brought around again?"

"Yes, it will be another wonderful morning to go for a ride. If anyone asks for me, tell them I am still sleeping. My grandmother worries so about me."

"And so she should, my lady. You ought to know better than to ride out by yourself so early in the morning. This is London. It isn't safe."

Elizabeth smeared her toast with marmalade and said, "Pish tush, Dulcie. It is nine o'clock, not early at all. What is more, it is not as if I am riding through Hyde Park. Green Park is very quiet. There are a few children and their nannies and some milkmaids, but other than that, it is just Parsons and me. So you see, riding in Green Park is quite unexceptionable."

"Parsons is a daydreamer, my lady. I wish you would get yourself a real groom, one who knows how to look after you properly."

Elizabeth smiled and shook her head. The one reason she kept Parsons on was that he was not a proper groom. He allowed her to go wherever she wished, at whatever speed she wished, and he never scolded her. Heavens! If Mr. Cochran knew how often she and Parsons got separated, he would give Parsons the sack! But the coachman didn't know because Parsons always returned to the gates of the park and waited for her to reappear. They then returned to the stables together.

Elizabeth smiled as she recalled how many adventures and interesting people had come her way during her solitary rides through Green Park. She did not, however, reveal this to Dulcie—nor to anyone else in the family!

"Which habit today, my lady?"

"The Devonshire brown, I think."

"Very good, my lady."

Elizabeth finished her breakfast and her toilette and went downstairs. The clock was chiming nine o'clock. Roberts opened the front door and watched her go down the steps. Parsons tugged at his hat and threw her into the saddle on her small chestnut mare. Then he climbed onto his old white cob, and they set off at a sedate walk.

When they reached the gates of the park, Elizabeth gave him a little wave and urged her mare to a canter. She loved to ride in the morning when the air was crisp. The gentle breeze ruffled her long, dark hair, and tugged at the net confection she wore as a hat. When they were out of sight of the children and the maids, she gave Cinnamon her head, and they sped across the ground at an exhilarating speed.

Finally, Elizabeth pulled back on the reins ever so slightly, and the well-behaved mare dropped to a trot. After another moment, they came to a small pond ringed with huge boulders. Elizabeth freed her knee and slipped to the ground. The mare cropped the grass, and Elizabeth sat by the pond and sighed.

She didn't know what it was about this year's Season. Perhaps it was having Penelope there, but somehow, she was on edge. Not in a bad way, she thought, but as if she were expecting something exciting to happen at any moment. She smiled at her reflection in the pool. Such silly daydreams from a mature lady.

She saw another reflection and whirled around to face Captain Sparks.

"Oh! You startled me!"

"I am sorry, my lady. I thought you heard me. I said your name twice. You must have been very deep in thought."

"Yes, I was," she said primly. "I often come here early in the morning to have a good think—by myself."

Gideon grinned at this, but did not take the hint. Instead, he sat down beside her and trailed his hand through the water, sending ripples across their reflections.

"A very wise thing to do, I suppose. Sometimes I think people don't do enough thinking."

"But you do, of course," she smirked.

"Lately, I have been thinking entirely too much. Between that and listening to others tell me how to behave, I hardly have time to be myself."

"A great loss," she murmured, then she gave a tiny gasp. "I do beg your pardon, Captain. That was very rude of me."

He merely smiled at her and said, "That's fair enough. I spoiled your morning. You deserve to take me down a peg."

"Perhaps, but I did not wish to offend you."

"No offense taken," he replied, gazing into her eyes. "I would like to think that we are good enough friends to be frank with each other."

Elizabeth shifted on the boulder so that she would not be looking directly into those dark eyes. Then she wished she had not turned because she could no longer tell if he was staring at her.

"Do you always rise so early?" she asked, turning back.

"It is hardly the crack of dawn," he said. "But yes, I do prefer to rise early. It is much more difficult here in London. The nights are much later than I am accustomed to. When I am on board a ship, though, I always follow the advice of Poor Richard."

"Poor Richard? You mentioned him last night. Who is he?"

"Just a fictional character," said the captain.

"Oh yes, the one your Benjamin Franklin created. So how does the saying go?"

"Early to bed, early to rise, makes a man healthy, wealthy, and wise." He gave her a self-deprecating grin and added, "I don't know how accurate it is." With this, he stood up.

Suddenly, Elizabeth did not wish for their time together to end, and she asked, "You do not consider yourself wise?"

"Not in the ways that are important in your world." He held out his hands to help her rise. They were standing inches from each other, face to face.

Her breath was shallow as she asked, "My world?"

He still held her hands, and she was shocked to find herself stepping closer. He was speaking, but his gaze was on her lips, and Elizabeth found it difficult to decipher his words.

Then she heard, and she snatched her hands back. Her eyes blazed as the captain continued.

"Yes, the world you should be getting back to. The world that would be rocked by scandal to learn that Lady Elizabeth had gone out without her attendant—something a lady never does."

"I assure you, Captain, I have an attendant. He is too well trained to be obtrusive, but do not worry. He is close by, so once again, you are safe from the horror of compromising me. You will not be expected to wed me!" she said tartly.

Elizabeth spun on her heels and grabbed Cinnamon's reins to lead her to the boulder so that she could mount. Strong hands went around her waist, and she was lifted effortlessly into the saddle.

When she looked down at him, she could see the amusement in his eyes, and she was tempted to lash out with her riding crop. Instead, she kicked the mare's sides and rode away.

"Same time tomorrow morning!" called the captain.

And with very unladylike spirit, she called, "In a pig's eye!"

Oh! What an infuriating man!

By afternoon, Elizabeth had regained her equanimity so that when her brother paid her a visit, she greeted him warmly. "Val! How fortunate that you have called."

The long-legged young man sat down in a spindly chair and asked affably, "How may I be of service, dear sister?"

Elizabeth smiled at him and said, "I have a favor to ask of you—a favor that is uniquely suited to your skills."

He straightened and leaned forward eagerly. "Interesting. You do not usually require the type of service I can offer. Who has offended you and how may I help you hurt . . . him? I assume it is a gentleman."

Elizabeth had the grace to blush, but she said, "Yes, but I am not certain gentleman is the right term. On the outside, perhaps, but he is too free and easy in his manners to be a true gentleman."

"Steady on, Sis. You could be talking about me, you know. Many people wonder if the word gentleman applies to me. Still, breeding is all that matters to the leaders of the *ton*. I suppose that is why I still have my choice of invitations each evening. But I am straying from the subject. Who is this alleged gentleman?"

"Captain Sparks. You have met him several times."

"Ah, the good captain with the colorful vocabulary."

Elizabeth frowned, and he chuckled. "He has been heard, on occasion, to let loose with the most inappropriate language. It will burn even the stoutest gentleman's ears. Tsk, tsk."

"Yes," she said. "I recall hearing such language one night, but to be fair, he thought no one was listening—well, no one but a groom."

"You intrigue me," said Val, watching her closely.

Elizabeth shrugged it off and said, "It was nothing. I was staying at Mimi's house and went over to Wintersford to get a peek at a new foal. I was not expecting to meet anyone, and had not dressed . . . well, I was not in my usual garb. He mistook me for a groom."

"I see, breeches and a smock, eh? Still, when one is born to noblesse oblige, one knows not to vent one's temper—and language—on the help. So, what is it the good captain has done to ignite your ire?"

"He is insulting."

Val pretended to reach for a nonexistent sword, and she put her hand on his and shook her head. "Nothing like that. It is quite the opposite, really. He has intimated that he has absolutely no designs on my person."

"Oh, so you are the one whose advances have been snubbed," he said with a wicked grin.

"Certainly not! *I* do not make advances."

"Of course not. A true lady would never do anything like that."

"Exactly."

"Well, not a lady such as yourself. Fortunately for me, there are other sorts of ladies. But I am straying from the point again. So tell me, what do you want me to do to Captain Sparks?"

"Find out about him, all that you can. I want to know the true reason that he and Avery have become such good friends. I want to know if he has a legitimate claim to being called a gentleman."

"Your wish is my command. And if I should learn that he is merely masquerading? What do you want me to do about it?"

"Nothing. Just come and tell me."

"Ah, so that you may have the pleasure of lowering the boom personally. Very well. I will consult with my associates this very afternoon."

"Thank you, Val. I knew I could count on you. Now, why did you call?"

"Oh, just for a visit. I felt a tug at my familial strings and wanted to see you."

"Shall I ring for refreshments?"

"No, I am too caught up in this new project." He rose and bowed over her hand. Then he snapped his fingers and said, "Oh, one thing. I may have to grease the palms of some of my less reputable associates, and that takes a supply of the ready."

"Certainly," she said, reaching for her reticule. Pulling out a substantial quantity of coins, she asked, "How much will you need?"

He opened his hand and said, "That should do. I will have something for you in a day or two."

When he had gone, Elizabeth sat back with a smug smile. If Val discovered, as she expected him to do, that Captain Sparks was an uncouth, penniless sailor—captain or not—then she would expose him to the rest of the *ton*.

A little voice urged caution. After all, he had saved Avery's life. She quashed the voice and said out loud, "I will teach the smug Captain Sparks not to trifle with me!"

Elizabeth put the captain out of her mind and pulled out her novel. She was soon engrossed in the tale. Not an hour passed, and she heard voices in the street outside. She hurried to the window and saw Captain Sparks exchanging words with her neighbor. Then he headed up the front steps.

Elizabeth flew to the drawing room door, catching Roberts just before he could open the front door.

"I am not in!" she said. "Not for anyone!"

The butler nodded and said, "Very good, my lady."

Elizabeth pulled the door closed, leaving the tiniest crack to spy through. He had changed from his riding gear and wore a bottle green coat with a striped waistcoat. His shoulders were so broad that she could not see all of them through the tiny gap.

Roberts accepted the captain's card and said, "Her ladyship is not at home this afternoon, sir."

"No matter. I did not come to see her ladyship. I came to see . . ."

"Good morning, Captain Sparks! How kind of you to call on us," said Penelope as she descended the stairs.

"Good afternoon, Miss Holloway. Actually, I came to call on your brother. Do you know if he is receiving?"

"Roger will be delighted you have come. I will take you to him."

"He mentioned last night that he would love to have the chance to examine some documents in the naval archives. If we can use one of Lady Elizabeth's carriages, I thought this afternoon would be the perfect opportunity."

"Oh, he will be pleased! Let's just go and tell him," said Penelope.

Elizabeth shut the door.

How silly of me! To think that I occupy his every thought! He is not even interested in speaking to me!

She returned to the sofa and took up her novel, but she failed to see the words printed on the page. She stood up and walked to the small escritoire in the corner. She should send a note to Val and tell him not to . . . but the captain *had* insulted her, several times.

Elizabeth heard the commotion of the captain's departure. She hurried to the window to watch as he lifted Roger Holloway in his arms, carried him down the front steps, and put him in the carriage. Then he oversaw the grooms as they secured the Bath chair to the back of the vehicle.

The captain turned to wave at Penelope, who was standing on the top step. His dark eyes were soft and kind—his smile alluring.

And then came the unbidden thought: *Why does he not look at me like that?*

Chapter Nine

"They are now placing wagers on who can win the silly chit," said Viscount Winters as he struggled to tie his cravat. With a growl, he tore the ruined one off his neck and put his hand out for another. "I tell you, when I heard that, I very nearly called them all out!"

Trying to calm the viscount, Gideon said, "Surely they do that sort of thing at the clubs over any number of young ladies."

Gideon was not overly concerned with what others thought of Elizabeth. He had been amused that morning in the park. He might have been more bothered if he had not seen Elizabeth peeking out the window of her house at him—both on his arrival and his departure with Roger. She might protest, but she was not unaffected by him.

"Yes, but this is different. I finally pried the truth out of Hazelton. If one of them can win her, he intends to ask her, announce the betrothal, and then break it off—very publicly!"

"You know that Wakefield is behind it," said Gideon, his eyes narrowing. "I know a couple of chaps who would be willing to . . ."

"No, you can't do that. The wagers have been recorded. Even without Sir Landon Wakefield, the scandal would continue. I shall have to warn her." Winters again tore the cravat from his neck and threw it on the floor. "Devil take it! You tie the demmed thing, Grimes!"

The viscount's valet hurried forward to take over the all-important task of tying a new cravat. When he was done, Winters nodded his approval.

"A stickpin, I think," said the viscount. The valet held out an emerald pin, and his master waved it away. "No, not that one, blast you."

When the valet offered a ruby pin, he accepted it. To Gideon's quizzical glance, he explained, "This S.O.R.E.S. . . ."

"Yes, I know, the Society of Rejected Elizabethan Suitors," supplied Gideon.

"Yes, well, they have taken to wearing emerald stickpins, cut in the shape of hearts."

"Emerald because of her eyes, I suppose."

"Precisely. Wakefield's idea, I have no doubt. I should have called the blackguard out the first time I saw him after Elizabeth rejected him. To think I used to call him friend. Hah! Elizabeth had the measure of Sir Landon all along!"

With deadly calm, Gideon said, "I could call him out, if you wish. To have to fly the country would be no great thing to me."

The viscount grinned and shook his head. "Good of you to offer, Gideon. However, we have other plans for you. Remember?"

His tone was perfectly dispassionate as Gideon said, "Still, it would be very satisfying to run him through. Not to sound vain, but I am accounted an excellent swordsman."

The viscount waited until his valet was out of earshot and said, "Perhaps after you and Elizabeth are wed. Tonight, however, we have a ball to attend—your first in London. Let us hope it proves fruitful."

On the threshold of the McKenzies' ballroom, Elizabeth smoothed her emerald green gown. It was styled simply with a single flounce at the hem and the requisite high waist. On a ribbon around her neck, she wore a large emerald surrounded by tiny diamonds. Her long hair was piled on top of her head, *à l'antique,* with short curls at each temple. She wore long silk gloves dyed to match her gown.

Penelope was no less elegant. Her gown was of silk in an antique bronze that glistened in the candlelight. She wore her mother's topaz jewels.

Lady Louisa smiled and took the girls by the arms. "Two such beauties. Each of you were so clever to have gowns made up to match your jewels. Very becoming. I shall be busy all night, helping you two fight off the gallants."

"Not that you will mind being surrounded by handsome men," laughed Elizabeth.

"I am so excited, Elizabeth, but it has been too long! And now, with the waltz. I do hope I don't faint."

"At the touch of a man?" laughed Elizabeth.

"It is practically an embrace," whispered Penelope.

Her friend was clearly apprehensive, and Elizabeth did her best to set her at ease.

"It is not anything like an embrace," she said with worldly confidence—not that she had experienced a romantic embrace herself. "You will see. There will be so much space between you and your partners that you will laugh at your missishness."

"I hope you are right. Look, there is your cousin. Oh, doesn't he look handsome?"

"Give me the dark good looks of Captain Sparks any day," said Lady Louisa with a sigh. At her granddaughter's look of surprise, she added, "If I were thirty years younger, that is. You must admit, my dear, he is a handsome man."

Elizabeth sighed, but she did not disagree. Instead, she said, "Come along. I see Grandfather standing near the entrance to the card room. Let us join him."

Elizabeth led the way and her two companions reluctantly followed. She curtsied to her grandfather, and he returned an elegant bow before kissing her cheek.

"Good evening, my child. Louisa, always a pleasure. And Miss Holloway. You look lovely. I did not have the chance to speak to you for very long last night at dinner. Are you enjoying your stay here in London?"

"Yes, my lord. Everything is so wonderful!"

"I am glad you persuaded that brother of yours to come, too. I spoke to him today. He had gone out with Captain Sparks. Your brother is such an interesting fellow. He has some ideas about how to help our displaced soldiers and sailors. I am trying to persuade him to speak to some of my friends in Parliament."

"I had no idea," said Penelope. "How kind of you."

"Not kindness, I assure you. If his ideas were implemented, I believe our society would benefit greatly. But there, I am talking politics to three beautiful ladies. I know you girls are itching to join the other dancers, and unless I miss my bet, these young gentlemen behind you are quite anxious to secure dances."

Elizabeth and Penelope turned around and were besieged by a cluster of gentlemen. Lady Louisa looked on with a smile.

"What about you, Louisa? Aren't you burning to join the dancers?" quipped the earl.

She rapped his arm with her fan and said, "There was a day, but alas, that is gone. And the girls can look after themselves. I think I will simply join the card players. I assume Cordelia is already within."

"Indeed she is, and quite pleased with her winnings so far," said the earl with a grin.

"What about you, Rotherford?"

"I don't care for cards, as you well know. I will just stay here and watch the dancers for a while. Enjoy yourself."

"Thank you. Oh, Rotherford, do come and signal me if Elizabeth and Captain Sparks should do anything extraordinary."

"Of course," he said with a chuckle. As she turned, he asked, "What do you consider extraordinary?"

"I don't know. With those two, waltzing together might be considered extraordinary."

He chuckled at this, and Lady Louisa entered the card room.

Gideon and the viscount watched the set that was in progress. It was a quadrille, and the steps called for the couples to circle around while turning this way and that.

After a few minutes, Avery said, "Have you noticed how many emerald hearts are glittering on the chests of the men here?"

Gideon replied gravely, "I have noticed."

"I am going to have to speak to Elizabeth about this. I don't relish the job," said the viscount.

Gideon nodded and said, "Perhaps you could merely watch who is the most persistent in his attentions and warn her away from him on some pretext. I hate for her to learn about Wakefield's betrayal."

"I will try. It is difficult, however. Warning Elizabeth away from someone should, by rights, be the task of her foolish brother. However, since that is not likely to happen, I will simply have to pluck up my courage and face her."

"Stout fellow," said Gideon, his eyes twinkling with laughter. "I would be happy to counsel her, but I doubt she would even believe me. As it is, she will probably demand to know why you are not warning her against me!"

The viscount grimaced and said, "I detest this sort of thing. Elizabeth can run rings around me in any argument." After a moment of gloomy reflection, he added, "If my grandfather were a more dictatorial sort, none of this would have come to pass. Elizabeth would have been safely married years ago, and I wouldn't have to intervene."

"Is that a complaint, my boy?"

Avery whirled to face his grandfather, his face turning scarlet. "Er, no, sir. Of course not."

"Rest easy, my boy. I half agree with you. But I

thought the great scheme was for the captain here to win Elizabeth. Surely you should be the one speaking to Elizabeth, Captain Sparks."

"It has nothing to do with the scheme," said Gideon. "Another matter entirely."

The earl did not look convinced, but he did not press the matter, thus giving the viscount time to collect himself.

"So how is the scheme progressing? Or is it?" asked the earl. He looked Gideon up and down and commented, "I see you are standing here talking to us, Captain, instead of dancing with my granddaughter. Not a very promising indication."

Gideon chuckled and said, "I admit things do not appear to be going well, but I have not given up. Slow and steady, you know."

"But not too slow," said the earl. "Sometimes, Captain, action, not caution, is called for. Now, if you will excuse me, I want to speak to Lord Fitzsimmons."

When they were alone, Winters said, "I will go over to the other side. That way, one of us should be able to attract her attention when the dance ends. If you get to her first, keep her here until I return."

Left on his own, Gideon watched Elizabeth with unabashed admiration shining in his eyes. She glanced in his direction and tossed her head in defiance. Gideon smiled.

At least she had noticed him. He recalled their heated exchange that morning in the park and smiled again. She might claim that she was indifferent to him, but she was lying. He seemed to have a very unsettling effect on her. Good or bad, he could not say for certain, but he planned to find out soon. Perhaps when they met at the pond in the park tomorrow morning. After all, she still owed him a kiss. Perhaps it was time to claim it.

The music finally stopped, and Elizabeth's partner guided her off the floor.

Gideon stepped in front of them, and said, "Excuse

me, Lady Elizabeth, but your cousin desires a word with you."

"Avery?" she said in surprise. Looking around, Elizabeth added, "If he wanted a word, he should have stayed put, shouldn't he?"

Another man wearing one of those emerald hearts stepped up and said, "My dance, Lady Elizabeth."

"Of course it is, Mr. Higginbotham. Captain, you don't mind telling my cousin that he will have to wait, do you?"

She started to pass, and Gideon touched her arm. She stared at his hand until he released her. Then she made the mistake of smiling up at him.

Their gazes locked, and Gideon said softly, "It is important. I am certain Mr. Higginbotham will understand."

"Only if the lady . . ." The young man trembled as he glared at the captain, but he stood his ground.

"It will take only a moment, Mr. Higginbotham," she said, smiling sweetly.

Elizabeth walked a few paces away from Mr. Higginbotham, and Gideon followed.

"What does Avery want? And where is he?"

Gideon looked over the heads of the crowd and said, "He is on his way now. Perhaps I can . . ."

He hesitated. He didn't wish to alienate her, but the musicians were already tuning up for the next dance—a waltz.

Avery had stopped and was chatting with someone. Higginbotham was coming toward them.

"Dash it all! Dance with me," said Gideon, taking her hand and leading her onto the floor as the music began.

He swept Elizabeth into his arms. With a gasp of outrage, she pushed him away.

Gideon smiled and held her tighter. "Not now, my dear. It would be most improper to desert me in the middle of a dance."

Fuming, she hissed, "I hope Mr. Higginbotham calls you out for this!"

"Oh, I wouldn't mind. I would then have the choice of weapons. Swords, of course."

Elizabeth looked into his dark eyes and saw the laughter lurking there. She smiled ever so slightly.

"What if I told you Mr. Higginbotham is an excellent swordsman?"

"I would be immensely relieved, since it is a dead bore fencing against an incompetent opponent."

"You are very sure of yourself, Captain."

He smiled down at her. "I have reason to be."

They danced in silence for several minutes.

Then Gideon said softly, "Fencing with you, however, is a great challenge. With every parry and thrust, I find myself in danger of being caught off guard."

Her eyes shining in amusement, she asked, "What nonsense are you spouting now?"

"Just that you persist in taking everything I say wrong. This morning in the park, for instance, I was not concerned for my sake. Rather, I was concerned for you. You are such a proud beauty, I would hate for the rules of Society to dictate to whom you give your heart."

"Even if the worst occurred, my dear captain, and I were forced to marry because of a perceived indiscretion, Society could still not dictate to whom I give my heart," said Elizabeth, all amusement fled. She licked her lips and said breathlessly, "But were we speaking of hearts this morning?"

"I was."

His heart was in his eyes as he gazed into her face. Pink tinged her cheeks, but Elizabeth didn't, or couldn't, speak, neither to ridicule him nor to confess her feelings for him—if she had any, and she was not ready to admit that she possessed any feelings for the good captain, save a certain amount of prickliness.

Finally, attempting to escape the situation with humor, Elizabeth said lightly, "The music should have ended when you said that, Captain. I don't know what to say."

"Don't say anything."

They continued in silence until the end of the dance. A fuming Mr. Higginbotham met them at the edge of the dance floor.

Gideon bowed to him and said, "So sorry, Higginbotham. I quite swept her off her feet. Here, you take her for this next one."

He took Elizabeth's hand and placed it on the other man's sleeve. Elizabeth glared at him and snatched her hand back.

Higginbotham was clearly confused as he stammered, "What? Well, I . . . thank you."

Gideon grinned and added, "Oh, by the way, I really like that stickpin of yours. I notice some of the other gentlemen are sporting the same one. Some sort of club sign?"

"No, no, it's uh . . ." The man flushed uncomfortably.

"It is in honor of the men who have returned from the war, Captain. Lord Falworth told me all about it," said Elizabeth.

"Men who returned from the war?" Gideon stepped closer to Mr. Higginbotham and said, "I am very happy to know all of you are wearing it for such a worthwhile reason and not as some sort of . . . jest."

"Of course not, Captain," said Mr. Higginbotham with a nervous smile. Then he said, "If you will excuse me, Lady Elizabeth, I have promised someone else the next dance. Perhaps later. Good evening."

Elizabeth rounded on Gideon, but he threw his hands up in mock surrender.

"What was that all about? What was . . . everything about?"

"Avery can explain. Ah, good, here he comes now." Gideon stepped out of the way to give the viscount a clear path.

"Avery Winters, what is this all about?" hissed Elizabeth.

"I'll tell you what it is all about, Cousin. Come with me so we may be private."

He took her arm, but she wrenched free and planted her feet firmly, saying, "I am not going anywhere with you. Say what you have to say and then leave me alone." Nodding at Gideon, she added, "And do not send your lackey after me again!"

"Really, Elizabeth, it would be better . . . oh, all right." The viscount lowered his voice and said, "There are men here tonight who are making game of you, Cousin."

"Fustian!" she said distinctly. Heads began to turn.

"Elizabeth, I vow that I am telling you the truth. You are the subject of a . . . prank."

"Avery, you are talking nonsense. These are my friends."

The viscount said sternly, "Elizabeth, since your brother sees fit to shirk his duty, it falls on me to warn you about this shocking plot against you."

"Plot? Against me?" Elizabeth stomped her foot and said clearly, "Avery, you have windmills in that head of yours! What rubbish! And to malign my brother, who is not even here to defend himself, is despicable."

"Nevertheless, Elizabeth . . . Elizabeth!"

The viscount reached for her, but she shook off his hand. Then Gideon captured her hand and spun her around. He ignored the gathering crowd. He ignored the viscount's frantic gesture for silence. All he could see was that the woman he loved was behaving in a most reprehensible manner.

Taking both her arms, he held on tightly and said, "Enough! All your cousin is trying to do, my dear Lady Elizabeth, is to tell you that all these men wearing little emerald stickpins in the shape of a heart belong to a unique organization called S.O.R.E.S.—the Society of Rejected Elizabethan Suitors. From what I understand, there are scores of members, and their sole object is to ruin you."

Gasps filled the immediate area. Men sniggered. Ladies clutched each other for support.

Gideon slowly released her, but he was ready to catch her if she should faint. Instead, Elizabeth threw out her chest, lifted her face to his, and slapped him as hard as she could.

"Jackanapes!"

"Shrew," he said softly.

Elizabeth laughed—that tinkling sound a woman can make that holds no amusement. Several people around them followed suit. Gideon sketched a bow, turned on his heel and strode away. The viscount fell into step beside him.

When they were in the hall, waiting for their hats, Avery said, "That was quite a scene. I daresay you have lost any chance of winning her favor now."

The look he received silenced him.

With hats in hand, they headed out of the door. After walking briskly for several minutes, the viscount again tried conversation. "This ball will be the talk of London by tomorrow. What are you going to do?"

Gideon stopped so quickly that the viscount skidded past and then turned to face his friend.

"Well?"

"Two things. Tomorrow morning, I will hopefully meet Lady Elizabeth in the park and mend my fences. If not tomorrow, then the next, and the next."

"And the other thing?" asked the viscount.

"I am going to find your friend, Sir Landon Wakefield, and call him out." Gideon strode off so quickly that the viscount had to trot to keep up with him.

"You can't do that," he said.

"Why not? He has insulted the woman I love. I cannot allow that."

The viscount gaped at him and managed to ask, "The woman you love?"

Gideon took a deep breath to clear his head. With a

shrug of his broad shoulders, he said, "I know that you think I agreed to this madness because I had no other choice. I was ruined, right?" To the viscount's nod, he laughed. "I agreed to this, my dear Winters, because I fell in love with your cousin before I ever met her. I fell in love with that damned portrait at Wintersford. I fell in love with all of your grandmother's stories about her, and Lady Louisa's stories. And now it is too late. I can't help it if she is a termagant, I love her!"

"But, Gideon, she is not yours to defend. I hate to be the one to tell you, but I don't think she will ever be yours after what just happened. And to call Wakefield out will only ensure Elizabeth's ruin."

Gideon considered this as he continued his walk toward the club. If he challenged Wakefield, he would not be satisfied with anything short of killing him. He did not really want to go to jail. But he could not let Wakefield's activities go unpunished.

He stopped again and found Winters eyeing him cautiously.

"Very well. I will not call him out. I will simply frighten him so badly that he will denounce his newly formed society and apologize to everyone concerned."

"How the devil are you going to do that? Wakefield's a proud man. That's what started all this in the first place."

"I have a plan. Come on. We're going the wrong way. Let's get a hackney. I have a couple of friends near the docks that I need to see."

"Now you are frightening me. You can't hire someone to murder him," murmured the viscount, but he followed Gideon all the same.

Elizabeth didn't know how she did it, but she made it through the evening. Her grandfather helped when he asked her to join him for the next set. It was a line dance, and they held hands as they performed the familiar steps between the line of couples. Wisely, he did not give her any words of sympathy. Pretending that nothing had happened made it possible for her to pretend that her world had not turned upside down.

They ended their dance, and her grandfather presented her to his friend, Lord Fitzsimmons, who also asked her to dance. Some of her other beaus, who were true friends, danced with her, too. If nothing else, the message was undeniable—Lady Elizabeth was both admired and well-protected. To offer an insult to her would likely lead down the road to social ruin.

What seemed like days passed, but finally the evening was over, and Elizabeth had danced and conversed without once losing her composure.

When she arrived home, she bade her grandmother and friend good night and sought her bed. She found pillows were very useful for absorbing the sound of her sobs.

Gideon didn't really expect Elizabeth to show up at the little pond. Not really. Still, he remained there for the better part of the morning. Finally, he gave up.

To work off his frustration, Gideon went to Jackson's Boxing Salon, looking for some poor soul to spar with him. Seeing the anger in his eyes, the other men avoided him. Then Valentine Lightfoot entered and sauntered up to him.

"Quite a night you had, Captain Sparks."

"Shut up," said Gideon.

The youth laughed and said, "Come on. You can relieve your vexation in the ring. I warn you, though. I may be light, but I am very quick."

They stripped to the waist and climbed into the ring. People began to gather. Here was Lady Elizabeth's brother, come to avenge his sister's honor against the man who had insulted her. Bets were placed surreptitiously.

Val bounced from one foot to the other as they circled each other. Finally, he bounced forward and delivered a light blow to Gideon's chin. Their audience cheered.

Gideon retaliated with a punishing blow to the young man's cheek.

"Not bad," said Val. "But can you do this?" He clipped Gideon just below the right eye and followed it with a blow to the stomach. Gideon attacked.

Picturing Sir Landon before him, Gideon was impossible to stop. His fist connected time and again, but Val took the blows and gave a few of his own.

Breathing hard, Val said, "It seems I am not fast enough. You're not hitting as hard as you can, though, are you?"

"You think I'm pulling my punches?" asked Gideon as he lashed out again.

"Perhaps, and I have to ask myself, why?" he added as he danced out of reach.

"Had enough?" asked Gideon.

"Almost," said the young man. With lightning speed, he closed in and landed a punishing blow to the stomach. Then again, he bounced out of reach. With a cheeky grin, he said, "Now I have. What about you?"

Gideon laughed and moved away. "Enough! You win!"

There was a rumble of disapproval from the onlookers as they settled their wagers.

Val walked over, shook Gideon's hand, and said, "Only because you didn't beat me to a pulp. I swear, if you had allowed yourself to truly let loose, I would not be standing."

"Perhaps. We will never know for sure."

"It doesn't really matter, does it? I mean, this is all a game," said Val as they left the ring. Glancing at Gideon sideways, the younger man said, "I do wonder why you held back."

"You are Lady Elizabeth's brother. I am already in her

black books. I would hate to think what she would do if I dismantled her little brother."

"So I live because of a woman. Fair enough! If only the ladies knew how much control they really have over us."

"Heaven forbid that they ever find out," said Gideon. "Will you join me for a drink, Mr. Lightfoot?"

"Val, remember? Thank you, but not now. I have kept one of my ladies waiting while we sparred. I must hurry to her side, or I will be . . . punished." Val said this with such a wicked grin that Gideon had to laugh.

As Gideon left the boxing salon, his mood was much improved. Perhaps he would see Elizabeth that evening.

After searching the faces at the Smyths' musicale and the Owens' rout, Gideon admitted that Elizabeth had not gone out that evening. He finally accepted the viscount's invitation to play cards at their club.

Several hours later, he went home, his head aching from too much wine and his pockets lighter.

Never mind, thought Gideon. *Perhaps my lady's temper will have cooled enough by the morning, and she will appear at our rendezvous in the park.*

He muttered a curse at his own folly. When had they ever had a rendezvous? He had happened upon her, and as far as he could tell, she was now avoiding that spot just as she was avoiding him. Not that he blamed her. Gideon wasn't particularly fond of himself either at that moment.

With a groan, Gideon climbed onto the bed, fully clothed, and fell asleep.

Elizabeth had slept off and on all day after the McKenzies' ball. The next morning, after tossing and turning all night, she did not wake until she heard the clock strike eleven.

Suddenly, she sat up. Eleven o'clock? She had slept too late to go riding!

Riding. She sank down on the soft mattress again. She couldn't go riding in Green Park. She supposed she would never go riding alone in the park again. After all, *he* might be there.

Or worse, said a mocking voice. *He might* not *be there.*

Despite his aching head, Gideon was at the park that morning. He felt a fool for going, especially when Elizabeth never showed up. Finally, he turned Roman toward the park gates.

"This is intolerable," he told the big horse. "We could wait there every day for a month before seeing her again."

The horse shook his head, and Gideon smiled. "You may be right. We need help, and I think I know someone who might be willing to help us. Lady Louisa will know if I still have a chance with Elizabeth. Yes, I know I don't deserve a chance, but a man has to have hope."

When he arrived at Elizabeth's town house, he was greeted coldly by the butler, Roberts.

"I would like to see Lady Louisa."

"I will see if she is at home, sir. Wait here."

None of this wait in the parlor for you, thought Gideon. *The butler has received his orders.*

A few minutes later, the butler ushered him into a tiny room at the back of the house that could best be described as a cupboard. There was hardly room for two people to stand in it.

The butler lit a single candle and then closed the door, saying, "Lady Louisa will be with you in a moment, sir."

"Thank you."

He looked around him and saw dust rags, some bottles on shelves, and two brooms.

A moment later, Lady Louisa bustled inside and shut the door after herself. Holding her finger to her lips, she whispered, "Sh. I don't want Elizabeth to know you are here."

"I'm sure the butler will tell her."

"No, I made him promise to be silent. He doesn't want Elizabeth hurt, either. So, you have made a fine mess of things."

"That is putting it succinctly," he replied. "Have I lost my every chance?"

"I don't know yet. She has not spoken of the incident at all. I was not a witness, of course, but I had it from Penelope after Elizabeth retired that night, and I went straight over to see Lady Rotherford the next day. Lord Rotherford was there, and he told me what he knew about the incident, too. Whatever made you do such a nonsensical—and public—thing? Elizabeth has every right to never speak to you again."

"I know, but I could not bear to see her making such a fool of herself. She ridiculed Lord Winters and his concern. She wouldn't even listen to reason—until I forced her to do so." He hung his head and said, "I have ruined my chances for good."

"Well, you did make her cry." He winced and she said, "After she made it through the entire ghastly evening, I heard her crying in her bedroom, but there was nothing I could do. She was not ready to be comforted."

Heaving a sigh, he said, "I am a cad."

"No, you are just in love with my granddaughter, and unless I am mistaken, Elizabeth has feelings for you, too."

He looked into those green eyes that were so like Elizabeth's, and he wanted to cry. She reached up and patted his cheek.

"We did not go out last night, but we are attending a small ball at Lady Chesterfield's house this evening."

"I will be there," said Gideon eagerly.

"No, it is probably best that you and Elizabeth do not meet just yet. Elizabeth needs to reassure herself that she is not going to receive the cut direct from people. Your presence would simply muddle the affair."

"I only want to talk to her and explain. Oh, what's the use? She hates me, and I can't blame her," he said.

"Do not despair, my dear captain. Give her another day or two to recover, and then you must try again. The next time, you should attempt to woo her, not annoy her. Understood?"

Gideon hung his head like a recalcitrant schoolboy and said, "Yes, my lady." Then he kissed her cheek.

"Oh, my! And I thought I was too old for a stolen kiss in the broom closet!"

"One is never too old for that!" he teased.

"Good-bye, Captain. Stay here while I make certain the coast is clear. I will tell Roberts when to let you out."

"Good-bye, Lady Louisa, and thank you."

Looking down from her sitting room window, Elizabeth watched the captain descend the front steps and ride away. Her heart did a strange little flip, but she refused to question why it might be behaving so strangely.

Why had he said those awful things to her? The question kept popping into her mind no matter how firmly she tried to quell it.

Their waltz had been delightful. She was secretly pleased that he had diddled Mr. Higginbotham out of his dance—especially after learning what those little green hearts were about. She sighed. At least most of the men who wore them had either left the ball or removed the pins after that awful scene.

How many had she seen at the beginning of the evening? She shivered at the thought. Perhaps when she was over the initial shock, she might let anger take over and plot some sort of revenge against those men. Until she completely regained her confidence, though, she would try not to think about it.

Elizabeth grimaced when she recalled that there had been only two callers that morning—Lady Yates and her sister, Mrs. Davenport—the two biggest gossips in London. She had somehow managed to pretend that she was not cut up by the incident, and they had left again, disappointed.

Would this afternoon be different? It would be unusual if her other friends did not come by to see her—out of curiosity, if nothing else. She had received only two bouquets of flowers in the past two days, too. Perhaps she was going to be ostracized for behaving so boorishly and for having her good name bandied about at the clubs.

Elizabeth shrugged. Scandals came and went so quickly. She was not truly concerned about her position in Society. She would come about.

In the meanwhile, a plethora of other topics buzzed around her head, and each one had at its center Captain Sparks. Gideon.

She tried it out loud. "Gideon Sparks. Captain Gideon Sparks."

With a tearful sigh, she whispered, "Gideon."

Just then, there was a knock on her door, and her maid entered.

"What is it, Dulcie?"

"Your brother has called, my lady. Shall I tell him you are indisposed?"

"No, send him up here to my sitting room. I do want to see him."

"Very good, my lady."

A minute later, Val entered and hurried to her side. He kissed her cheek and sat down on the stool in front of her chair, his knees practically under his chin.

Elizabeth shook her head and laughed. "Silly, take that chair."

He slipped into the chair and held up his hand. "I do not need to tell you, my dear sister, that I know all about the other night. Really, slapping the good captain!"

"You weren't even there," she said.

"One did not have to be in attendance to have heard the entire tale—blow by blow, so to speak."

"Oh, Val, it was awful. He was awful, and what was almost worse, so was I. I lost my temper. If I had not done so, it would not have blown up in my face like that."

"Elizabeth, you should not blame yourself. You were provoked. Besides, I have the very solution for you, right here in my pocket." He took a paper out of his coat pocket and placed it in her hands. With a wicked little grin, he said, "Read it out loud."

The notes were in Val's wide scrawl, written in pencil. "Gideon Sparks. Captain of the American ship the *Resistance*. Former first mate on the privateer *Southern Winds*. Made captain at five and twenty. Sank the British ship *English Lady*, 1812."

She paused and Val said, "That's right. Roger Holloway's old command."

Crumpling the paper, Elizabeth said, "But we already knew that. Gideon and Roger have become fast friends since they met here."

"Gideon? Are you so close to the man that you call him by his Christian name? I find myself wondering exactly why you wanted this information, Elizabeth. I mean, I thought you wanted ammunition to ruin Captain Sparks. Was I wrong?"

"Oh, I don't even know any more," she said.

"Well, continue reading. You may find that you hold the answer to your dilemma in my notes."

She smoothed out the paper and said, "Very well. Let's see. Sank the *English Lady* . . . owned two ships until last year, when one sank in a sudden storm off the coast of the West Indies. Recently lost his other ship in a freak accident. Punishing right cross?" Elizabeth paused with a puzzled frown on her brow.

Val said, "Oh, that's just a little comment on his boxing ability. Go on. You haven't read the best part yet."

"Saved Avery Winters' life. Lost everything. Penniless, but has no tailor's bills, no stable bills. Doesn't pay his rent. All accounts are sent to Lord Rotherford for payment."

Val smiled at her like the cat that swallowed the cream.

"What does it mean?" she whispered.

"It means, my dear sister, that Captain Sparks is really a Captain Sharp."

"I don't believe that."

"Oh, you can believe it. Until your grandmothers took him in hand . . ."

"My grandmothers? What do they have to do with . . . oh, no."

"Yes, I think there is a bit of matchmaking going on. But the point is, Captain Sparks is nothing—well, certainly not the wealthy gentleman he now portrays."

"Oh, Val," groaned Elizabeth.

He grinned at her. "And so the tables have turned. Now you have him in your hands, what are you going to do with him?"

"I don't know, Val. I really don't know. I should be furious with Mimi and Grandmother, but I am not. I should be anxious to expose him to Society, but again, I am not. I don't know what is the matter with me. I am not usually so indecisive."

"No, you aren't." He studied her for a moment and then smiled. "Could it be that my big sister has finally found a man to say yes to?"

"Val!" she whispered, her cheeks turning pink. "Oh, Val," she said miserably, "I think it just might be."

"Then I will say congratulations, my dear, for I know that if you want the man, you will have him. And I will say this for the good captain: I like him. I can't say that about the others who have courted you." He kissed her on the forehead and rose. "Let me know if I can be of any further assistance. I have several very delicate enterprises filling my days—and nights—at the moment, but you have only to send a note, and I will come as quickly as possible."

"Thank you, Val."

When he had gone, Elizabeth wandered to the window and gazed at the street below. Somehow, the scene looked different. The sunlight was brighter, more cheerful.

Her smile disappeared, replaced by a frown.

How was she ever going to get the captain to come up to scratch when she wasn't even speaking to him? And did she truly want him to do so? He had said he would meet her at the pond in the park. She had avoided riding for the past two mornings because of it. Somehow, she was certain he had been there.

Might he try one more time?

The smile reappeared at the mere possibility. She hurried into her bedroom and called for Dulcie.

"Dulcie, please fetch my new riding habit, the mulberry one. I plan to wear it tomorrow morning, and I want to be certain it fits properly."

"Yes, my lady."

While she waited, Elizabeth glanced at her image and blew herself a kiss.

"What is this all about?" asked her grandmother as she followed Dulcie back into the room.

Elizabeth grinned and shook her head. "I cannot say, Mimi. It is a secret. Well, not so much a secret as it is a possibility. Until I know how things will end, I do not wish to talk about it."

"Oh, that makes everything clear."

Chapter Ten

Crack! Slam!

Oh, but that felt good! thought Gideon. He dodged Sir Landon's fist and then planted him a facer.

Panting, Sir Landon wiped blood from the corner of his mouth and said, "You're insane, Sparks! What the devil gives you the right to kidnap me?"

"The right of honesty and fair play," said Gideon, not even breathing hard. "Two things you know nothing about."

"Give 'im another one to th' chin again, Cap'n!" shouted Guinny, his henchman.

"Attaway! Screw up 'is ogle!" shouted the other ruffian.

Gideon stumbled backward as Sir Landon's fist connected with his nose. Blood streamed down his face, but he charged again, catching his opponent in the breadbasket.

Wakefield fell back and was still. After a moment, he pushed himself up on one elbow and again wiped his mouth.

"What the devil do you want from me?"

"I want you to apologize to Lady Elizabeth—in public. Then you will ask her—no, beg her, for a dance."

"She will never accept," said the young man, sitting up and feeling his swollen jaw.

"That is her prerogative. Personally, I hope she slaps your face and kicks your . . ."

Sir Landon winced and asked, "Why do you care? Don't

tell me she has wound you up in her web. It will never do, you know. The romp will only break your heart."

"So you are saying Lady Elizabeth broke your heart? You have a very strange way of behaving toward the woman you love."

"You mean my little society?" He had the audacity to laugh. "I heard how she believed that folderol about those emerald hearts being worn for the war heroes. Rather ironic." He started to rise, but the look in Gideon's eyes made him shrink down again.

"Look, Sparks, Elizabeth only got what she deserved!"

"No one deserves what you have done. Your pride was hurt, but instead of taking it like a man, you have resorted to the lowest sort of vengeance."

Sir Landon glared at him and said, "I will enjoy watching you squirm, Sparks, while she has you in her web. And when she sends you off to lick your wounds, you will be begging to become a member of my society."

Gideon reached down and plucked the man up by the cravat.

His face inches from Sir Landon's, he growled, "Keep your opinions to yourself and remember that I will be watching. If you fail to follow my instructions . . ."

"All right, all right. I'll do it."

Gideon released his cravat, and Sir Landon stumbled backward.

Wiping his mouth, he mumbled, "I never meant for it to go this far anyway. It was just a lark."

"I don't see it that way."

"Yes, I have come to understand that."

Sir Landon scuttled out the door of the rustic cottage.

Sticking his head back in the open door, he demanded, "How the devil am I supposed to get back to London?"

"Keep your shirt on," said Gideon. Turning to his two henchmen, he handed them a small purse of coins and said, "Excellent work, gentlemen! You are both well worth your pay. There's a little extra in there!"

"Thank you, Cap'n. If you should ever need us again, you know where to finds us," said Robbie, pulling on his forelock.

"Only not t'night," said Guinny. "We'll be too busy celebrating!"

"Drink one for me," said Gideon, picking up his coat and shrugging into it.

Guinny paused at the door and said gruffly, "You be careful with yourself, Cap'n. Snakes like that fellow have been known to strike when yer not expectin' it."

"Thank you, Guinny. I'll be careful." When the ruffian still lingered, Gideon asked, "Was there something else?"

"Jus' this. Watch out with the lady, too. I don't like t' think o' you, well, you know." He shuffled his feet.

"I will be especially careful with the lady," he promised. "Now, take our guest back to town and have a good evening."

The man tugged at his hat and nodded. Then he joined his friend on the seat of the old cart. Sitting in the back, Sir Landon looked away as they drove off.

Gideon glanced around the cottage to be certain that he hadn't forgotten anything. As he closed the door, it fell off its hinges. No matter, he thought. It had served his purpose.

If only he could put things right with Elizabeth as easily. Lady Louisa had said they would attend the Chesterfields' ball that night. Gingerly, he felt his jaw and wiggled it back and forth. He really wasn't in any shape to attend a ball. Besides, he had promised Elizabeth's grandmother to give it another day before pursuing her.

With a curse of disappointment, he swung up on Roman's back and headed for the nearest inn to drink the night away.

* * *

"I don't see very many of those dashed emeralds tonight," commented Lady Louisa to Lady Rotherford as they entered the Chesterfields' ballroom that night.

"Good thing. Rotherford was ready to kill the puppy."

"Captain Sparks?" exclaimed Lady Louisa.

"Not him! The other one—Sir Landon." They continued to watch Elizabeth and Penelope as they danced. After a moment, the countess added, "For twopence, I would have let him do it, too. Impudent mushroom! I am very glad our Elizabeth did not wed the man."

"Sir Landon," said Louisa for confirmation. She made a moue at her friend's look of disdain. "Oh, I know, but you are not being very clear, Cordelia."

"I should hope not. This ball is so quiet and poorly attended, there are ears everywhere! It surprises me. I thought there would be more people hoping for another scene like the other night. I know for a fact that Lady Chesterfield was very busy this afternoon, paying calls to let everyone know that the infamous Lady Elizabeth had accepted her invitation and would be present tonight. Perhaps the farce was not so widely spread as we . . ."

"Lady Rotherford and Lady Upton. So glad you could attend my little soiree," said Lady Chesterfield with a smug smile.

"We would not miss it, Lady Chesterfield," said the kindhearted Louisa.

Lowering her voice slightly, their hostess smiled and said, "Of course not. One has to do everything one can when a reputation is threatened. It doesn't do to let them think you are afraid to show your face."

"Oh, is that how it works?" asked Lady Rotherford. "I have never experienced such a thing. I do remember your daughter—the younger one, I believe. That was quite the talk of the town, wasn't it? Still, you survived it. It must have been a great relief when he agreed to wed the chit."

"Well, I . . ."

"Of course, people never were convinced that she ended up with the actual father, were they?" added Lady Louisa.

Lady Chesterfield left in a huff and the two friends laughed quietly.

"That will teach that old bulldog to toy with us," said Lady Rotherford.

"You were magnificent, Cordelia," laughed Lady Louisa.

"You were quite good yourself, Louisa."

They watched in silence as the dance ended, and the girls' next dance partners presented themselves. Elizabeth appeared completely at ease. No one would have guessed that her nerves were stretched to the breaking point.

"I sent a note round to Avery, warning him to keep the captain away tonight."

"Yes, I spoke to the captain myself. I do hope, however, that Elizabeth does not see his absence as a rejection."

"Better for her to think that she has given him a disgust of her than for her to have the opportunity to give him the cut direct. They need a little distance."

Lady Louisa sighed and said, "I thought things were going so well. I can tell you, he is very cut up about it. I begin to doubt that they will ever make a match of it."

"Well, there is always next year. Perhaps someone else will take her fancy."

"Yes, I suppose so," said Lady Louisa. Perking up, she added, "Elizabeth did mention going to Paris in the fall. Perhaps she will find a handsome Frenchman."

"Heaven forbid! And if heaven does not, then I will! A Frenchman? One of those émigrés who has finally gone home now that we have whipped Bonaparte? Not for Elizabeth!"

Louisa chuckled and asked, "But an American is acceptable? We have fought them, too! And been beaten twice."

"Yes, but an American who comes from English stock!

That makes him acceptable." After a moment, the countess said, "Anyway, I have grown quite fond of Captain Sparks. I was rather looking forward to being able to bully him like I do the rest of the family."

"Perhaps you will still get the chance, my dear," said her husband, who appeared at her elbow.

He kissed his wife's cheek, and she teased, "You see, Louisa. I told you it was too quiet in here. Anybody might overhear our confidences."

Louisa, however, was more interested in the earl's comment than her friend's witticisms. "What do you mean, Rotherford?"

"I spoke to one of my friends, who happened to see Sir Landon returning to town late this afternoon in an old cart driven by a couple of ruffians. He was sporting a black eye and a swollen jaw. Unless I miss my guess, our captain has had words with Wakefield."

"I am glad to know that someone has. He deserves anything he gets after making up that silly club about our Elizabeth," said Lady Louisa.

"At least it saves me from having to call the man out. Pistols I can still manage, but I don't know that I am up to swordplay."

"You would never be so foolish," said his wife.

He looked down at her with steel in his eyes and said, "I would not be able to sleep nights if I thought he had gotten away unpunished. But the captain—or someone—has taken care of the young fool for me. I intend to speak to Captain Sparks and see if it was he."

Elizabeth and Penelope joined them, and they turned the conversation.

"Are you ladies enjoying yourselves?" asked the earl.

"Oh yes," said Penelope. "It is so much more pleasant tonight. It is more like the assemblies I used to attend at home. There is more room to dance."

Lady Louisa and the countess exchanged amused glances.

"Yes, Lady Chesterfield must be delighted," remarked the countess with a smirk.

"What about you, Elizabeth?"

"I am fine, thank you, Grandfather," she said, looking at the door for the hundredth time since their arrival.

With a bright smile, Penelope said, "Look, there is Lord Winters."

Eagerly, Elizabeth looked toward the entrance to the ballroom. Avery waved and headed their way, but he was alone. She heaved a sigh and looked away.

Lady Louisa touched her granddaughter's arm and said, "Here comes Lord Mowery, Elizabeth. Such a fine young man, don't you think?"

"Good evening, Lord Rotherford. Ladies," said the handsome young earl.

They all smiled at him, even Elizabeth. He had been present at the other ball, but he had not been wearing one of those emerald hearts.

"How is your sister, Lord Mowery?" asked Lady Rotherford.

"She is very well, thank you. She recently presented the marquess with an heir, you know."

"Yes, I had heard. I know your parents must be pleased. The first grandchild. Such a joy."

He smiled, and Elizabeth said, "The music is starting again." Elizabeth took his arm, and they returned to the dance floor. A large case clock stood by the wall next to the door. Elizabeth wondered how soon she could leave.

She watched as Avery led Penelope onto the floor. Penny was gazing up at her cousin with adoration. He, too, appeared to be enjoying himself.

Elizabeth forced herself to concentrate on her partner, but it was not easy. Now that she knew it was unlikely that Gideon would attend the ball, she only wanted the evening to end.

With every step of the waltz, Elizabeth wished it were Gideon who was holding her. She was not certain how things would work out. Truthfully, she had no idea if the captain was affected by her, but she was eager to put it to the test. Tomorrow morning, she promised herself. The thought that he might not appear at the pool in the park made her shudder.

"Are you feeling all right, my lady?" asked Lord Mowery.

"Just a little fatigued," she said.

"Would you prefer to sit down?"

"No, no. I love to waltz," she said with a smile.

The last thing she wanted was an intimate tête-à-tête with Lord Mowery.

If it were with Gideon, that would be another matter entirely.

The next morning, Gideon was dressed before he decided that it was not worth the trouble going to the park. Elizabeth was not going to be there. He was wasting his time.

What he really wanted to do was get roaring drunk again. That, however, was not a viable option. *What good would it do? What good would anything do?* he thought glumly.

Mallard entered, and Gideon said, "Pour me a brandy, will you? A large one." The servant poured it and Gideon added, "Just bring me the bottle."

"Very good, sir. Did you want me to order your horse brought over from the mews, sir?"

"No, I have decided not to go out after all."

Mallard watched him drink down the contents of the glass. "Will there be anything else, sir?"

"No." Gideon filled the glass again. Looking up, he gave the valet a wry grin and said, "If anyone should call, tell them, as you people say over here, that I am not in."

"Very good, sir."

The butler retreated and closed the door.

Gideon set the glass on the table. He was not twenty

years old anymore. He knew that he could not drown his sorrows with drink. The night before had proven that when he had imbibed much too freely at that inn. Now, he had a sore head and still had not solved anything.

Taking out a deck of cards, he dealt a game of patience. Two hours later, the door opened and Mallard hurried inside.

Taking the glass from the table, he said, "I know you said you did not wish to be disturbed, Captain, but Lord Rotherford is here to see you!"

"Rotherford?"

He began tidying his master's cravat until Gideon slapped his hands away.

"Leave me alone, man! And show the earl in."

"But sir, in your condition . . ."

"What condition? Good grief, man, I am not drunk. Show him in."

Mallard went to the door and threw it open. "Lord Rotherford."

Gideon stood up and offered his hand. After the slightest hesitation, the earl shook his hand.

Glancing at the game laid out on the table, Rotherford said, "Black knave on the red queen."

"So it is," said Gideon. He circled the table and indicated the leather sofa. "Will you be seated, my lord?"

The earl sat down on one end and Gideon asked, "Would you care for a brandy?"

"Nothing for me," said the earl, glancing over his shoulder at Gideon. "I would like to speak to you, Captain Sparks."

"I assumed so, since you have called. What is on your mind?" Gideon sat down on the other end of the sofa and turned to face the earl.

"A friend told me he saw Sir Landon returning to town late yesterday afternoon. He was not in the best shape, and he was being driven by a couple of rough customers in a rickety dogcart. You wouldn't happen to know anything about that, would you?"

"I did not see the spectacle myself," said Gideon, his dark eyes giving away nothing.

"I see. He was rather bruised, too," said Rotherford.

"Poor fellow. Must have taken a tumble."

"Possibly. Personally, I was relieved. I was preparing to call the beggar out. Didn't much relish the possibility, what with Sir Landon being some thirty years younger than I am."

"I shouldn't think so. Sometimes it is better to leave matters to the younger set," said Gideon. "Are you certain you would not like a drink, sir?"

"Perhaps I would," he replied.

Gideon got up and poured both of them a glass.

When he handed it to him, Rotherford lifted it and said, "To the younger set."

Gideon smiled, but he did not join him.

With a little grunt of satisfaction, the earl rose and said, "I do hope we will be seeing more of each other, Captain. I was speaking to my secretary the other day about the benefits of owning a ship to transport our raw wool to the United States to the manufacturers there and then bringing their cotton back to England. He thought it was an excellent idea."

Having difficulty keeping his hopefulness in check, Gideon simply said, "Interesting."

"We would not move on it too quickly, of course. But by fall, I should think we could put our venture into operation."

With a smile, the earl grasped Gideon's hand and gave it a firm shake.

He turned to go, but Gideon, never one to live on false hopes, said, "This venture, my lord, I assume it is connected to the success of another scheme already in place."

The earl shook his head and said, "No. If I did not

have confidence in the venture, and with everyone involved in it, I could not endorse it. Whether the other 'great scheme,' as my wife calls it, succeeds or not, has nothing to do with my business plans."

Gideon grinned ear to ear and shook the earl's hand again. "I am glad to hear that, my lord, very glad indeed."

The earl looked at him intently and added, "For personal reasons, Captain, I hope that my wife's plan does succeed. I think you would be a very good addition to the family. I also think you could make my granddaughter happy, and that, my dear boy, is a subject very close to my heart."

"I will do my best, sir."

"See that you do. But I have kept you long enough. You probably have many important things to do." With a glance back at the game of patience, the earl chuckled and left the room.

Gideon waited a moment and then called for Mallard. "Send to the stables! No, wait. Never mind. I will go myself."

"Very good, sir," said the surprised servant.

Gideon started out the door, but he spun around and asked, "How do I look? Is my cravat straight? My coat? Oh, forget it. It doesn't matter! Wish me luck!"

"Good luck, Captain!" called the valet.

Gideon lost no time in riding to the pool. It was almost noon. He could not believe he had wasted the entire morning on a silly card game.

Over and over, he muttered, "Let her still be there. Let her still be there."

Then he turned Roman toward the hidden pool, holding his breath as it came into view.

Nothing. No one.

His shoulders slumped. His good mood collapsed around him like dust. With a sigh—he didn't even feel up to saying a few oaths—he slipped to the ground.

"Idiot," he said.

Then he spied three little wild violets, their stems twisted into one. He picked them up. They were still alive!

Gideon grinned and said to the horse, "She was here, old boy! I know she was here!"

He swung up on the broad back and turned toward Mayfair and Elizabeth's town house, whistling all the way.

When he arrived, the scene was one of bustling activity. A large black traveling carriage stood at the door. At first, he feared that Elizabeth was packing up and moving back to the country, but a moment's observation showed that servants were carrying bandboxes inside the house, not loading them in the carriage. He wondered who had arrived.

Gideon hesitated. Now was not the time to rush inside. Elizabeth was busy with whoever it was and would have no time to listen to his declaration—if he was even ready to make a declaration, he cautioned himself. After all, just because Elizabeth had gone to the pond, it did not necessarily follow that she was in love with him. Why, they had hardly even shared a private conversation. No, he should retreat and see her later, when things had quieted down.

A voice drew his attention, and he looked back at the carriage.

"Please see if you can find it, Mary. It is the only needle I have, and I really don't wish to go to the shops today."

The lady was dressed in black from the top of her head to her toes, and she was wringing her hands as the servant searched the ground. Just then, she looked up. Their eyes met.

Gideon smiled. There was no doubt that this lady was a close relation to Elizabeth and Lady Louisa. She had the same startling green eyes. He dismounted and hurried to join the search. With his keen eyes, he spotted the golden needle and took it up the steps to the lady in black.

"I believe this is yours, Lady . . ."

"Mrs. Lightfoot. How kind of you to help, sir."

Gideon swept a bow and said, "Captain Sparks at your service, madam. I am a friend of your, uh, mother."

"Please, Captain, won't you come inside so I can thank you properly over a cup of tea?"

"Another time, perhaps. You and your family will wish to visit in private."

As he kissed her hand, he spied Elizabeth watching them from the drawing room window. "Good day, Mrs. Lightfoot. I hope you enjoy your stay."

"Thank you, Captain," she said, turning away.

With no regard for propriety, Gideon looked at Elizabeth and blew her a kiss. She looked a little shocked. And then she smiled. With a nod, Gideon swung up on Roman's back and rode away.

"Mother, I am delighted you have come to stay. We are a little crowded. You remember that Penelope Holloway and her brother are staying with me."

"I suppose I could go to a hotel," said her mother.

"No, my dear girl, we can't have that!" exclaimed Lady Louisa. "When was the last time I had my daughter and granddaughter all to myself? I cannot even recall! You will stay in my room with me."

"That is silly, Mimi," said Elizabeth. "I will share with Penelope. She will not mind in the least. I will tell Roberts at once."

"If you are certain, my dear?" called her mother as Elizabeth hurried out of the drawing room.

"I suppose I should have waited to send a letter, hear from Elizabeth, and then come, but that seemed much too involved," said the usually organized Mrs. Lightfoot.

"There is no need for that," said her mother with a

wave of the hand. "We are family, after all. How is Mr. Lightfoot?"

"He is in a bit of a state. He does not approve . . . but there, I should not divulge his opinions. He was quite amenable by the time I left home." She glanced around the empty room and said softly, "I think he is worried about Valentine, too."

"But Val is a delightful boy," said Lady Louisa.

"I know you think so, Mother. You are his grandmother."

"Yes, but I hear the nicest things about him. Hostesses are always happy when he attends their little parties. He is so obliging with the young ladies—pretty or not, it makes no difference to him. And if you need him to take some old dear as a partner at cards, he complies with the sunniest of smiles. I am quite proud of our Val," said Lady Louisa.

Her daughter gave a grimace of a smile, but she made no comment. Patting her hair, which was twisted into a tight chignon, she said, "I would like to wash the dust of the road from my hands and face. Do you suppose my things have been taken upstairs yet?"

"If not, you may use my room, Lilian. The first door on the right."

"Thank you, Mother."

Lady Louisa sat back with a sigh. When Elizabeth entered, she rolled her eyes and said, "I don't know if I can stand one of your mother's visits right now."

With a giggle Elizabeth said, "But we are always complaining that Mother never visits us—especially without *him.*"

"I know, I know. We will just have to make the best of things."

"Oh dear. We were supposed to go the theater tonight."

"We can forget that. She will never countenance going to such a spectacle. I think we should not even ask her."

Elizabeth recalled the kiss that the captain had just

blown at her and pouted. "Any other time, I would have been delighted to have her show up unannounced. Oh well, we must try our best to see to it that she enjoys her visit. Otherwise, it might be her last."

"I agree," said Lady Louisa. An irrepressible twinkle lit her eyes and she added, "Precisely how do we do that when she is opposed to every sort of entertainment that London has to offer?"

Elizabeth snapped her fingers—an unladylike gesture that would have brought an immediate reprimand from her mother—and crossed the room to the small escritoire in the corner. She opened it and flipped through the invitations there. She turned and flourished two or three cards at her grandmother.

"A musicale, a poetry reading, and a picnic."

"Yes, but she will want to leave when the dancing starts at the picnic," said Lady Louisa.

"Then we will take two carriages, and she can come home early."

"Clever girl," said Lady Louisa.

Desperate girl, thought Elizabeth. How was she ever going to bring the captain up to scratch if she could not see him? There had to be a way!

After attending the theater that night, Penelope wandered into the room she now shared with Elizabeth and sat down by the fire. She stared into the flames with a dreamy expression on her face.

Elizabeth, who was reading in bed, asked, "What has happened to you, Penny?"

Penelope glanced up, and Elizabeth could see that her eyes were shining. She climbed out of the bed and hurried to her friend's side, sitting down on the little stool at Penelope's feet.

"Tell me everything," she breathed.

"Oh, Liz, I don't know where to begin. We were in the

box at the theater. I was very glad that Miss Baldwin was able to go with me. She is a dear, you know, but she does tend to fall asleep when she sits down."

"Very convenient for you," teased Elizabeth.

Penelope blushed, and pursed her lips. Elizabeth put a finger to her lips and crossed her heart.

"Your cousin and the captain arrived."

"Oh, my mother has a great deal to answer for," muttered Elizabeth.

"Lord Winters was wearing a dark blue evening coat with a scarlet waistcoat. He looked so handsome," she breathed.

"What about the captain?"

"He looked nice, too," she said. "We chatted while waiting for the curtain to open. By the time it closed again, Miss Baldwin was sound asleep. I was afraid her snoring would wake her."

"And where was the captain?"

"He had grown bored with the play, so he left the theater. Oh, Elizabeth. Lord Winters took my hand and gazed into my eyes. I thought my heart would burst! Do you know how many years I have wished and dreamed of that very thing?"

Elizabeth smiled. Penelope had fancied Avery since her come out all those years ago. He had been naught but a callow youth, but she had fallen in love with him on the instant.

"I know, my dear," she whispered, taking her friend's hands and giving them a squeeze. "What happened next?"

"We stayed where we were all during the interval—afraid to move lest we wake Miss Baldwin. We were sitting toward the back of the box and no one saw us and called on us. We might as well have been alone."

"What did you talk about?" asked Elizabeth. Never having been in the situation, she was puzzled to know what people in love talked about for endless hours.

"Anything, nothing. Mostly, Avery—I mean, Lord Winters—talked. Did you know he wants to take a larger part in running your grandfather's estate? He reads every word about sheep and cattle and improving the land."

"I had no idea. I thought he only wanted to go back to America and oversee that."

"Oh, he liked it, but since he has returned, he said, he has found England much more to his liking. He said there are too many things here that are dear to his heart."

"Avery said that? Do you think he was talking about . . . you?"

She nodded and quelled a little squeal. "Oh, Elizabeth! I am so happy! I never dreamed my life could take such a turn, and all because of you!"

"Me? What did I do? You should be thanking Roger. All I did was provide a place for you and Roger to stay so he could do his research," protested Elizabeth.

"You don't think I fell for that story, do you? Roger may have done a little research while he has been here, but the real reason I am here is because you wanted it. Thank you—from both of us!"

Elizabeth smiled and hugged her friend.

Growing serious, Penelope said, "Not a word of this to anyone! Nothing is settled, you know. There is no guarantee that . . ."

Elizabeth said, "Pish, tush! You know Avery will come up to scratch. It may take him some time, but he will. Mark my words." Suddenly, she grinned and said, "We will be like sisters! I will finally have a sister!"

Again they giggled and hugged.

Then Penelope said, "But I haven't asked about your evening, Liz. Did you and your mother and grandmother have a pleasant chat?"

"It was . . . nice," said Elizabeth. "It has been a long time since the three of us have sat down together.

Mother still does not approve of our merry way of life, but she managed not to irritate my grandmother too badly. We have persuaded her to attend a musicale and even a picnic. She refused the poetry reading, however."

"In heaven's name, why?"

"She fears the tone of today's poetry is too full of innuendoes about . . . love." Elizabeth laughed and said, "She is probably right about that."

Elizabeth yawned and Penelope said, "We should go to bed. Will you play lady's maid for me?"

"Of course," she said, rising and helping Penelope remove her gown and put on her night rail.

When they were in the big bed, and the candle had been extinguished, Penelope whispered, "I think I am too excited to sleep."

Elizabeth said, "Try. Something tells me that the next few days are going to be very . . . exciting. Good night."

Chapter Eleven

The next morning, Elizabeth dressed in her mulberry habit one more time and rode her mare to the park. Just to be certain that Parsons would not interfere, she urged Cinnamon to a brisk canter as soon as they entered the gates. Parsons, on his old cob, followed along after them at the usual plodding walk.

Elizabeth's heart was pounding in her chest as she rode. She was so afraid that Gideon would not be there, and almost more afraid that he would be. What would she say to him? More importantly, what would he say to her?

Stop this, she told herself. *It is all Penelope's talk about love and offers that has me so unnerved. Captain Sparks and I are friends. Nothing loverlike has passed between us, and there is no reason to think anything will today.*

Try as she might, however, Elizabeth could not erase the sunny smile from her face.

She entered the clearing, and her heart did a strange flip.

Gideon was there! When he saw her, he kicked out of his stirrups and hopped to the ground so that he might catch her by the waist as she dismounted. A sudden shyness came over her, and Elizabeth quickly moved away from his touch.

Her voice was breathless as she said, "Good morning, Captain Sparks."

"Good morning, Lady Elizabeth. What a lucky coincidence that you chanced to ride in this direction today."

"As I mentioned before, I often do so."

What is the matter with me? she asked herself. *I can speak to the Prince Regent without difficulty, but I am acting like a green girl with Gideon.* She flushed at the thought of misspeaking and using his Christian name.

Gideon took her hand and led her to the large ring of boulders. Elizabeth sat down and began to feel much better with something solid beneath her.

He sat beside her and said, "Your cousin is in quite a state."

"Avery?" He nodded and she commented, "About Penelope, you mean. Yes, she is in quite a state, too."

After several moments when the silence threatened to overwhelm them, Gideon finally spoke again. "Was that your mother I met yesterday?"

"Yes, she has come for a visit. It doesn't happen very often. It was good of you to find that needle for her. She is an ardent needlewoman."

"I was happy to help. I thought I might call this afternoon to meet her properly, if that is all right with you."

"Yes, that would be fine."

"Elizabeth . . ." he began. Her eyes flew to meet his dark gaze. "I haven't had a chance to apologize to you for the other night. I hope you know that what I said was because . . . for your protection. I did not mean to cause you any pain or . . . problems. I hope you can forgive me."

Elizabeth smiled at him, "You are already forgiven. Am I?"

"But, my dear Elizabeth, you did nothing that warrants an apology. It was all my fault."

"I behaved abominably to you. I . . . I slapped your face."

She lifted her gloved hand and stroked his cheek. He caught her hand and kissed it. Leaning forward, their knees touched as his arm went around her.

"Come on, you old nag," said Parsons, dragging back

on the reins to get his cob's nose out of the grass. "Oh, there you are, m'lady. Good mornin', Cap'n."

Gideon was already on his feet as he gave a hearty, "Good morning." Under his breath, he added a grumbled, "You miserable cur."

Elizabeth giggled, but she said, "Parsons, why don't you go on and start back to the gate? I will catch up to you in a minute."

"Yes, m'lady," said the servant, dragging at the reins to make the stubborn old horse turn around.

With a shy smile, Elizabeth said, "Any other day when we get separated, he never catches up to me."

Gideon took her elbows and pulled her closer. Looking into her eyes, he said, "I know, and we have so much to talk about. When can I see you alone again?"

"I don't know. With my mother here, my time is even more . . . oh."

She gave herself over to his kiss. It was deep, passionate, and full of promise. It was also agonizingly short.

"Go, before I forget myself and make you forget yourself."

"But, Gideon," she protested as he turned her around and gave her a tiny push.

"Time enough for that later. Let me help you mount."

He threw her into the saddle with no effort at all. Leaning down, she said, "The Beauchamps' picnic tomorrow. Will you be there?"

He grinned at her and sent her mare off with a little pat on the rump. He called after her, "Wild horses could not keep me from it!"

Elizabeth kept her gaze on Gideon until Cinnamon had carried her out of the clearing and back to normalcy.

She touched her lips, recalling that kiss—that delicious, promising kiss.

* * *

Elizabeth arrived home to find Val just entering the house. When she called out to him, he turned, looking at her absentmindedly. Parsons helped her dismount and led her mare away. Elizabeth hurried up the front steps.

"Val, what is it? You look a fright."

"Not now," he said, his eyes darting up and down the street. "Let us go inside."

"Of course. I suppose you are come in answer to Mother's summons."

"What? Oh, quite," he said, handing his hat to Roberts. "I should speak to her. I need to thank her for the money—long since gone, but that is neither here nor there," he muttered.

Elizabeth was busy removing her gloves and did not comment on his remarks. "I must go up and change, Val. I am sure you will find Mama in the drawing room. Go right in."

Elizabeth hurried up the stairs to the room she was sharing with Penelope. She threw off her clothes and washed her face and hands before stepping into the pale yellow morning gown Dulcie was holding out for her.

"I think I will wear the pearls," she said. The maid brought the pearls, and Elizabeth held them up to her neck. "No, not the pearls. The topaz, perhaps."

"The topaz? They have such a heavy setting," ventured the maid.

"True, but what else is there?"

"There's this package that came this morning from Rundell and Bridges. Perhaps whatever you bought there might be suitable," said the maid.

"Rundell and Bridges? The jewelers? But I haven't been in that shop in . . . oh, yes, now I remember," she lied as her fingers ripped into the wrapped package. Inside was a small card which she hid in her palm as she opened the box, which held a necklace of gold filagree with an intricately carved ivory rose in the center.

"It is perfect, my lady."

"Yes, it is," said Elizabeth. "Put it on me, Dulcie. My fingers are trembling."

The maid looked at her strangely but did as she was bid. Against the background of her pale yellow gown, the effect of the delicate rose against her creamy skin was stunning.

"It is perfect for this gown, my lady."

Elizabeth waited impatiently for Dulcie to smooth her hair and then dismissed her. She turned over the small card and read the brief note.

At your service, always.

Gideon

Her heart did that strange flip again. She took the card and placed it in the silver trinket box on her dresser. Rising, she gazed at her image in the glass and smiled. What a perfect day this was!

Downstairs, Val was holding court as he entertained his mother with the mildest *on-dits* from the social whirl. Over her mother's head, Elizabeth's gaze met Lady Louisa's; her grandmother rolled her eyes. Penelope giggled at this, and Roger frowned.

"Your brother has just been telling me about the riotous lives some people live here in London, my dear. I had forgotten how silly people can be. Why don't you ring for tea, Elizabeth?"

"I will, Mama," said Val, getting up and giving the bell rope a hearty yank. He turned back to the ladies and said, "And then, if I may drag Elizabeth away for a few minutes, I would just like to have a word with her, in private."

Roberts entered immediately and Elizabeth's mother said, "We would like some tea and refreshments, Roberts."

"Very good, my lady," replied the butler.

"*Madam* will do very well for me, Roberts."

"Very good, madam," said the butler, closing the door again.

Lady Louisa turned to her daughter and said, "Lilian, you should not try to reform the help. He knows that you have the same rights to the title of 'Lady' as I do."

"But, Mother, Mr. Lightfoot prefers not to use his title and so do I. It does not bother me in the least. I would hope you are not so shallow as to let it bother you."

"That was not my point," said Lady Louisa. "With the servants . . ."

"Val and I will be back in a moment," announced Elizabeth.

Each of the two older women clamped their lips closed tight. With a slight shrug of her shoulders, Elizabeth shot an apologetic glance to Penelope and Roger.

"What do you want to do first while you are here in London, Mrs. Lightfoot?" asked Penelope.

"The only thing I really want to do is visit the mercers' shops and see their selections of threads. I have been working in gold thread for some time, but I understand they also have other metals such as copper and brass."

"I would be happy to go with you," said Penelope. "I enjoy needlework, too."

"Thank you, my dear. It is always more pleasant to share such an experience. And afterward, perhaps we can stop at a bookstore. I would like to find a new book of sermons to take home for my husband."

"Val, how do you get yourself into these scrapes?" asked Elizabeth.

Her brother completed another circuit of the dining room, the only room they could find that was not in use or being cleaned. He raked a hand through his dark curls and shook his head dolefully.

"I don't know, Lizzie. I mean, all I wanted to do was help these ladies. Then they started talking to each other and found out about me, and us, and . . . oh, it is a mess," he moaned.

He returned to take the seat beside her and clutched her hands. "You have to help me! Now Lady Yates has confessed all to her husband, and I have heard it from friends that he is looking for me to call me out! I didn't even dare to go home last night!"

"Val! How awful!"

"And do you know the most ironic thing of all?"

"I am afraid to ask," said Elizabeth.

"I haven't even . . . I mean, we—Lady Yates and I—have never even . . . you know."

"Never even . . . oh! Val, how do you get yourself . . . oh, never mind. We have been over that road already. What can I do to help? Do you need money?"

"I always need money," he said with a wry grin. "But that isn't the main thing, Lizzie. I need a place to stay. If I stay with one of my friends, it is bound to get out. Yates will discover my whereabouts, and I will be forced into accepting a challenge."

"And we don't want that," murmured Elizabeth.

"I certainly do not, especially since I have done nothing . . ." At her piercing stare, he amended, "Almost nothing to earn a challenge. Besides, Yates is a good man. I don't want to kill him, and he's too fat to really fight me. He will challenge, and I will choose swords because I know better than to say pistols. I certainly do not wish to die!"

"Val, the problem is, I simply don't have any more room in the house. You know Penny and Roger are staying here. And now Mother."

"Look, I don't care. I'll sleep in a cupboard if I have to."

"Why don't I give you a bank draft and send you off to a hotel, or maybe to Paris?" asked Elizabeth.

He appeared to consider this and then shook his head. "No, perhaps later, but for now, I simply must lie low. Yates is combing the city for me. If I took the draft to your bank to cash it, he could very well see me."

"Then you must go back home. You need not tell your father . . ."

"No! I refuse to go! I would rather die in a stupid duel than go home and listen to my father's jaw-me-dead sermons from morning to night."

"Then I don't see what is to be done," said Elizabeth.

She heaved a sigh. So much for looking beautiful when the dear captain called to be properly introduced to her mother. Elizabeth was already exhausted from the problems laid at her feet.

"Please, Lizzie, you have to help me."

"Come on. We should get back to the drawing room before someone comes looking for us—I meant Mother," she added when he looked around as if expecting Lord Yates to materialize through the walls. "Let me think for a few minutes."

He grabbed her hand and kissed it, saying, "You are the best of sisters!"

She shook her head and led the way back to the drawing room.

As she opened the door, she froze in amazement at the tableau before her.

Avery was there, down on one knee in front of Penelope. All eyes were glued on him as he said, "Penelope Holloway, I love you with all my heart! Please, will you be my wife?"

Penelope fell off the chair and into his arms, knocking him over and kissing him fervently as they rolled on the floor.

Her mother gasped in horror, her grandmother gasped in joy, and Roger burst out laughing.

Blushing and sputtering, Penelope and Avery came to their senses and clambered to their feet.

Val hurried past Elizabeth and began pumping the viscount's hand. Elizabeth hurried to hug her friend.

Finally, it grew calmer, and Roger said, "Doesn't anybody want to ask me if I consent to my sister's alliance with the viscount?" All eyes turned on the man in the Bath chair.

Avery stammered, "Well, I thought . . . I mean, Penelope is not so young that . . ."

Roger laughed and said, "Of course I agree . . . if that is what you want, Penny."

"Oh, yes, Roger! Yes!" She hurried to her brother's side and kissed his cheek.

"Then it is settled?" asked Avery.

"I think it is," said Roger, giving his sister's hand to Avery in a symbolic gesture. "It's about time she got married and out of my hair."

Everyone laughed except Elizabeth's mother, who still appeared stunned. Elizabeth could tell that her mother would never view Penelope in the same manner.

With a sigh, she pulled Avery to one side and said, "A word in your ear, Coz."

"What is it? If you're going to ask if I have told Grandmother, the answer is no. It is none of her business whom I wed. And by God, after the merry dance you have had, neither she nor Grandfather had better say a word to me!"

Elizabeth chuckled and said, "Take a breath, Avery. I was not asking that. I was wondering if you might ask Penelope and Roger to come and finish out their stay in London with Grandmother at Rotherford House. It is just that Val suddenly finds himself without a roof . . ."

Avery stopped her and said, "Say no more. I know all about Yates. He asked me on the street this morning if I had seen my cousin. I explained that Val is not really my cousin. Let me send a messenger to Rotherford House, and I will gladly take both Penny and Roger away with me this very afternoon."

"Thank you, Avery. You have relieved my mind considerably."

"What is Val going to do?"

"He promises that he only needs a place to hide until everything blows over—a week, at most."

"I think that is one promise I would want to have in writing," said Avery.

Elizabeth laughed at this and then said, "Thank you, Avery, And congratulations to you. I couldn't be more pleased."

"Thank you, Elizabeth. I hope that someday I will be saying the same thing to you," he said.

"So do I," she whispered as he returned to his fiancée's side. "Val, the problem is solved. Write a note to your landlord and one of the servants will go and fetch your things."

"Thank you, Elizabeth. I knew you would work things out!"

As Val hurried out, Roberts entered and announced the captain. Elizabeth colored prettily as she greeted him.

His eyes on the necklace she wore, Gideon said, "I hope I am not intruding, my lady."

"Not at all. Welcome. Let me present you to my mother. Mother, this is Captain Sparks, the man who saved Avery's life."

"How do you do, madam?"

"Captain Sparks," she said. "I am glad you have called so that I might thank you again for finding my needle. Come and sit by me."

Avery announced his and Penelope's betrothal, and congratulations were offered. Lady Louisa went upstairs for a nap. While Penny and Roger went off to pack, Gideon sat by Elizabeth's mother, listening dutifully as she explained every golden stitch in the altar cloth she held in her lap. He looked over at Elizabeth from time to time, but remained politely attentive.

Finally, he said, "I really should be going."

"Must you, Captain?" asked Elizabeth, rising also.

"Yes, I have another call to make. It has been a pleasure meeting you, Mrs. Lightfoot."

"And you, Captain Sparks. Thank you again for finding that needle. I intend to visit the shops as soon as possible to purchase several extras."

"A wise decision," he remarked.

"Let me walk you to the door," said Elizabeth.

As they strolled slowly toward the drawing room door, he whispered, "I knew that would look lovely on you."

"Thank you, Gideon. It is beautiful."

"I hope it was an appropriate gift," he added. "It is for your birthday. It's coming up soon, isn't it?"

"Yes, next week."

She continued by his side as he entered the hall. The front door loomed, and Elizabeth said, "You will be there tomorrow, won't you?"

"The park at nine and the picnic after that," he said softly, his eyes speaking of the love in his heart—or so she believed. She smiled at him, and he took her hand to bow over it and kiss it lightly.

"Until tomorrow," she whispered.

He nodded and left.

Elizabeth turned to find that the hall was empty—neither the butler nor a footman in sight.

Dear Roberts, she thought. He was such a clever servant!

With this, she hurried up the stairs to help Penelope pack.

Gideon spent the evening with his conscience. It was a wrestling match of epic proportions, but he thought he had finally won by the time he had finished his last glass of brandy and fallen asleep on the sofa.

He had decided that he would tell Elizabeth in the morning that he was penniless. He suspected that she had made inquiries, but he was not certain. Besides, she needed to hear the truth from him.

Then, if she still appeared to be interested, he would ask her to marry him.

Please God, let her say yes.

On this thought he had fallen asleep.

As for Elizabeth, she tossed and turned in the large bed that she had shared with Penelope only the previous night—Penelope, whose every hope had been fulfilled that very afternoon.

Her evening with her mother and brother—her grandmother had defected to Rotherford House for the evening—had been painfully long and dull as she watched the clock tick slowly.

She heard the clock in the hall strike midnight. Elizabeth turned over once more. The sound of a door opening sent her to the hall, but no one was about. Then she heard the front door close. Hurrying back to her room, she looked down on the street and saw Val striding away.

The fool! she thought, wringing her hands. He had promised he would not go out at all, that he would not even leave the house. Yet there he went, putting himself in danger. If Yates should find him and call him out . . . it didn't bear considering.

Elizabeth climbed back into her bed, wishing for the dawn when Val would be home and safe and she could go to the park and melt into Gideon's embrace, forgetting all her troubles.

In the gray hour before dawn, Elizabeth awoke with a start. After glancing around her room, she closed her eyes.

Before she sank into sleep again, she tried to recall what had aroused her. A sound, that was it—the sound of her door closing. She struggled to open her eyes again. No one was there. She was all alone.

At this, the thought of waking one day and finding

someone with her in bed made her shudder with delicious anticipation. Then she frowned.

There had been something else. A voice. Val's voice.

Throwing the covers off, Elizabeth sat up.

I may never see you again. That was what he had said. Dear God! He was going to meet Yates on the field of honor! She raced down the hall to his room. Perhaps it had been a dream. His bed was rumpled and empty, but there was a hastily scrawled note on the dressing table.

She tore it open and then crumpled it in horror.

Elizabeth rushed back to her room and stood there, wondering what was to be done. The note said the duel was to be at Wimbledon Commons! Could she get there in time? Would she be able to stop it?

Without calling her maid, she struggled into a simple gown, all the while praying she would not be too late. Already a plan was forming. She would go to Gideon's rooms in St. James Street. He would know what to do.

Twenty minutes later, she hopped out of the hackney cab and dashed toward the building where Gideon and Avery had rooms. She had sent servants to Avery's rooms before, but as she stood in front of the building and wondered which was Gideon's door, she hesitated. Taking a deep breath, she decided it was the door on the right. She knocked . . . and knocked . . . and knocked.

Finally, Gideon himself opened the door. His valet wandered up behind him.

"Elizabeth! What the devil are you . . . come inside quickly!"

"Gideon, it's Val!"

"Val? What about him?"

"He has gone to fight a duel. We have to stop him!" she cried.

"Calm down. It doesn't do any good to panic. Now, come in and sit down over here." He led her to a chair near the adjoining room. "Tell me everything while I am getting dressed. Mallard, go next door and rouse Lord Winters."

The valet nodded and disappeared.

Quickly, Elizabeth told her tale, glancing from time to time to the open door, beyond which she could hear him dressing. "So you see, I know he has gone to Wimbledon Commons and that he thinks he will probably not be coming back. I don't know if he meant . . . oh, Gideon, I am so frightened," she sobbed as he returned, fully clothed and booted.

He took her in his arms and kissed her forehead. The door opened and Mallard entered.

"Lord Winters is not in, sir. I roused his man, but he said his lordship was staying the night at Rotherford House."

"Gideon! What are we going to do?" asked Elizabeth.

"Wimbledon Commons, Mallard, where is it?"

"Go north, sir, in the same direction as that inn you visited the other night."

Heading toward the door, Gideon asked, "Is the hackney still waiting?"

"When I first went next door, I took the liberty of sending to the stables to fetch your horses. You can travel faster on horseback."

"Good, then we will be on our way." As he spoke, he ushered Elizabeth out of the room and down the short flight of stairs to the street.

Without a word, Gideon threw Elizabeth into the saddle. He knew better than to offer false hope.

As they neared the Commons, Gideon said, "That must be it, that group of men over there."

"What is all the noise about?" asked Elizabeth. "Are duels usually so loud?"

Gideon helped her dismount, and they hurried toward the disturbance, where the most unusual sight met their eyes.

"Is that a . . . baguette he has in his hands?" asked Elizabeth.

One of the onlookers laughed and said, "A long piece of bread, it is, but it was longer when they started. This is the second piece, too."

"What the devil is he doing?" cried Elizabeth.

Gideon laughed and said, "I suppose Val has chosen his weapon. He should have thought to have Yates fight with one, too." Elizabeth shot him a look of scorn, and he fell silent.

Just then, Yates lunged, and Val parried with his slender loaf of bread. As the tip flew through the air, Val dropped the end and began running from the angry husband, around and around in an ever-widening circle.

Sick with fright, Elizabeth moaned, "Gideon, you have to do something!"

The two continued in their circle. As they passed, Gideon stuck out his foot, tripping Lord Yates. The baron went down, and Gideon leaped upon him, his knee on the man's chest. He wrenched the rapier from the baron's grasp and threw it aside.

The breath had been knocked out of Lord Yates, and as he gasped for air, Gideon hissed, "Have you lost your senses, sir? Do you not see what a fool you are making of yourself?"

"I'm . . . going . . . to . . . kill him," he managed to say between gasps for breath.

Gideon shook his head and said softly, "Not today, you're not, not with his sister looking on."

Yates glanced at Elizabeth and groaned.

"I know how it is, my lord, to love a difficult woman."

"How can you know? You're not even married."

"Doesn't mean I haven't suffered similarly." He looked up at Elizabeth and grinned. Returning his attention to Yates, he said, "Surely there is a more dignified way to end this than dueling with a youth who has been nothing but a pawn in Lady Yates's hands. She only wanted to make you jealous."

"How do you know that?"

"Val told me," he lied. Elizabeth's eyes grew large at this, and she looked away. "The best thing you can do would be to take her away on a trip, perhaps to Paris."

"I've been wanting to go to Paris," grumbled the baron.

"There, you see."

"But I can't leave things like this. Everyone thinks my wife and Lightfoot . . ."

Gideon climbed off the baron and extended his hand to help the man rise. "Val, come here."

The handsome young man hurried forward. He was hardly mussed at all, while the baron looked completely done in.

"You will apologize for the, uh, misunderstanding, will you not?"

"Of course, only too happy to do so," said Val.

"In front of everybody here," said Yates.

"If you like," said Val. Then, raising his voice, he said, "I am sorry we had this misunderstanding, Lord Yates. It was all my fault, and I apologize."

Lord Yates frowned at Val and then said, "Well, I suppose that will do. It wouldn't be right for me to hold a grudge. Apology accepted."

Val and the baron shook hands, and suddenly, the small group of men—Lord Yates, the seconds, the surgeon, and several others who had been present when the challenge was issued—dispersed.

"Captain, thank you for coming to my rescue," said Val.

"You don't mind if I don't say that it was a pleasure."

The young man laughed and said, "Not at all."

"But it is your sister you should thank. She is the reason I am here."

Both men turned to Elizabeth. She was perched on a

fallen log, her face in her hands. Gideon hurried to her side.

"Elizabeth, are you all right?"

She nodded and attempted a smile. It was a very poor effort, but her brother didn't appear to notice as he said, "Lizzie, I don't know how you managed, but I do appreciate your bringing the good captain."

She sighed and said, "You're welcome, Val. But please, do not do this again."

Grinning from ear to ear, he crossed his heart and said, "I promise never to let you know about a duel of mine."

"So comforting," said Elizabeth.

"Well, I am for town. I suddenly have an enormous appetite. I would offer to take you two back with me, but I am riding with Huffy Whitson, and there isn't room in his high perch phaeton. Good-bye."

"Our horses will be fine," said Gideon.

Suddenly, it was quiet, the way nature was supposed to be just after dawn.

"Shall we go?" he asked, pulling her to her feet.

"Yes. Thank you, Gideon, for everything."

He put his arm around her, and she leaned her head on his shoulder as they strolled toward the horses.

When they were both mounted, Gideon said, "I was over this way last week. There is an excellent little inn in the opposite direction from London. They have wonderful food."

Elizabeth perked up and said, "Any sort of food would be heavenly, Gideon."

Soon, they were sitting in the private parlor of a small inn, a large breakfast laid out on the table in front of them. When they were both full, Gideon led her to a sofa that was in front of the fire. Rain had started to fall outside and the wind was howling through the trees.

"A terrible day for travel," commented Gideon.

Elizabeth snuggled against him and his arm went around her shoulder. "It would be criminal to take those poor horses out of the barn on a day like this," she remarked.

Gideon twisted around so that he could look into her eyes—the eyes he had fallen in love with two months earlier.

"I love you, Elizabeth."

She smiled and kissed his lips. "I love you, too." When she would have kissed him again, he pushed her away and held her at arm's length.

"I have to tell you something, and I will understand if what I have to say changes the way you feel about me."

She appeared worried as he began to speak, but soon her brow cleared, and she kissed him once more.

"Is that all?" she whispered.

"All? I have just told you that I am no better than a fortune hunter. I may have been sanctioned by your relatives—oh, and that is a story you will have to hear—and you may care for me, but the truth is the truth. I am penniless, except for a little bit I have saved since arriving in London, and that is money from your family. Now what do you have to say?"

Elizabeth leaned in closer and closer while Gideon tried to draw away. Finally, he fell over backward on the sofa, and Elizabeth tumbled on top. They slipped to the floor with her straddling him.

"As I said before, I love you, Captain Sparks. It doesn't matter how much money you have or don't have. I love you."

He kissed her thoroughly then.

Finally, he pulled away enough to ask, "And you will marry me, as quickly as possible?"

"This very moment, if I could," she giggled.

A crash of thunder shook the inn, and Gideon said, "I think we may be stuck here—not just all day, but all night, too."

"How dreadful," she murmured, kissing him yet again. "But, darling, your reputa . . ."

Elizabeth pushed up on one elbow and snapped, "If you dare to say one word about not wanting to compromise me, Gideon Sparks, I shall kick you!"

With a lazy grin, he said, "Well, we cannot have the bride doing that to the groom." He slipped out from under her and stood up. Elizabeth watched him hurry to the door.

"Gideon?" she whimpered.

He put his finger to his lips, and opened the door.

"Landlord! My wife and I will be staying the night. Ready your best room. My wife is not feeling well, and she needs to go straight to bed."

"Very good, Captain," said the landlord.

Gideon closed the door and returned to Elizabeth.

Helping her rise, he pulled her close and whispered, "Prepare to be compromised!"

Epilogue

One week later, their lips a bit bruised from nights and days of passion, Elizabeth and Gideon returned to London. Mrs. Lightfoot had taken to her bed in shame. Mr. Lightfoot had arrived and was prepared to take his stepdaughter to task for her scandalous behavior.

Lady Louisa and Lady Rotherford welcomed both of them with smug smiles and open arms. Lord Rotherford presented the pair with two wedding presents—a new ship for Gideon to do with as he pleased and a special license issued by his friend, the bishop.

The very next day, St. Paul's Cathedral sparkled with candles and the jewels of the *ton*. Elizabeth wore one of her favorite gowns, cream-colored to match the ivory necklace around her neck. Gideon was resplendent in a morning frock coat with tails.

When the vows had been said, Sir Landon Wakefield threw up his hands and said loudly, "I hereby declare that the Society of Rejected Elizabethan Suitors is dissolved!" The congregation erupted in laughter and cheers.

When the bishop had silence again, he finished the marriage service and told Gideon that he might kiss his new bride. The entire congregation roared with laughter as Lady Elizabeth forgot their presence and kissed her groom with great passion, proving to one and all that Lady Elizabeth was anything but cold!

About The Author

Julia Parks resides in Texas with her husband of thirty-plus years. She has three wonderful children, two delightful sons-in-law, and three beautiful grand-children. When not writing or doing research for her novels, she teaches French at a nearby high school. Along with reading and writing, the author enjoys cross-stitch, quilting, and playing the piano. Most of all, she enjoys playing with her grandchildren.

She welcomes comments from her readers and can be contacted at Kensington Publishing or by e-mail: authorjuliaparks@yahoo.com.

BOOK YOUR PLACE ON OUR WEBSITE AND MAKE THE READING CONNECTION!

We've created a customized website just for our very special readers, where you can get the inside scoop on everything that's going on with Zebra, Pinnacle and Kensington books.

When you come online, you'll have the exciting opportunity to:

- View covers of upcoming books
- Read sample chapters
- Learn about our future publishing schedule (listed by publication month *and author*)
- Find out when your favorite authors will be visiting a city near you
- Search for and order backlist books from our online catalog
- Check out author bios and background information
- Send e-mail to your favorite authors
- Meet the Kensington staff online
- Join us in weekly chats with authors, readers and other guests
- Get writing guidelines
- AND MUCH MORE!

Visit our website at
http://www.kensingtonbooks.com

More Regency Romance From Zebra

__**A Daring Courtship** 0-8217-7483-2 **$4.99**US/**$6.99**CAN
by Valerie King

__**A Proper Mistress** 0-8217-7410-7 **$4.99**US/**$6.99**CAN
by Shannon Donnelly

__**A Viscount for Christmas** 0-8217-7552-9 **$4.99**US/**$6.99**CAN
by Catherine Blair

__**Lady Caraway's Cloak** 0-8217-7554-5 **$4.99**US/**$6.99**CAN
by Hayley Ann Solomon

__**Lord Sandhurst's Surprise** 0-8217-7524-3 **$4.99**US/**$6.99**CAN
by Maria Greene

__**Mr. Jeffries and the Jilt** 0-8217-7477-8 **$4.99**US/**$6.99**CAN
by Joy Reed

__**My Darling Coquette** 0-8217-7484-0 **$4.99**US/**$6.99**CAN
by Valerie King

__**The Artful Miss Irvine** 0-8217-7460-3 **$4.99**US/**$6.99**CAN
by Jennifer Malin

__**The Reluctant Rake** 0-8217-7567-7 **$4.99**US/**$6.99**CAN
by Jeanne Savery

Available Wherever Books Are Sold!

Visit our website at **www.kensingtonbooks.com.**

More Historical Romance From

Jo Ann Ferguson

__A Christmas Bride	0-8217-6760-7	**$4.99US/$6.99CAN**
__His Lady Midnight	0-8217-6863-8	**$4.99US/$6.99CAN**
__A Guardian's Angel	0-8217-7174-4	**$4.99US/$6.99CAN**
__His Unexpected Bride	0-8217-7175-2	**$4.99US/$6.99CAN**
__A Rather Necessary End	0-8217-7176-0	**$4.99US/$6.99CAN**
__Grave Intentions	0-8217-7520-0	**$4.99US/$6.99CAN**
__Faire Game	0-8217-7521-9	**$4.99US/$6.99CAN**
__A Sister's Quest	0-8217-6788-7	**$5.50US/$7.50CAN**
__Moonlight on Water	0-8217-7310-0	**$5.99US/$7.99CAN**

Available Wherever Books Are Sold!

Visit our website at **www.kensingtonbooks.com.**